The Empty Room

Brooke Linford

Prologue

I blasted the air conditioning onto my flushed face. In the rear view mirror, a cherry-coloured forehead reflected back. Taking the curves with ease, I ran through what I'd say to Mark, how I'd bring up last night.

As I rounded a corner, I swerved to avoid a Landcruiser parked halfway across the road. 'Move over, dickhead,' I mumbled, hitting the accelerator. The trees flashed by in a blur of green and brown as I approached the highway that headed to home, but the blast of a horn from behind caused me to tap my brakes and glance into the mirror. The Landcruiser. I frowned, easing my foot onto the brake as behind me the driver flashed their lights and blared the horn again. The trees were thick here; there was no place to pull over to let him pass. But I crossed the left line and tried to slow the car as the Landcruiser bore down. Gravel sprayed under my wheels and, clenching my teeth, I prayed the tyres would hold. 'Arsehole!' I screamed.

But it was too late.

The Landcruiser's bull bar loomed large in the rear view

mirror. A bump from behind. The wheels spun out. Trees loomed.

Then the crunch of metal into wood.

Shattering glass.

Thump of airbag into my face.

Silence.

Silence so loud it hurt.

A car door slamming.

Hands cupped against a broken window.

Blonde hair.

A familiar giggle. 'Whoops.'

Pain hit. Fast and hard. I wanted to claw away the airbag, but I couldn't move. I struggled to peer into the face at the window, the cupped hands. But the person was gone.

I was alone.

Tasting blood, I opened my mouth and screamed.

Chapter 1

The bathroom was hot as I scrubbed the sink. Hands red and sweat dripping down my back, I hunched forward, keeping my eyes down, keeping my eyes averted from the pregnancy test waiting on the window ledge.

Instead, I glanced at the clock on my phone. I still had time to kill.

Dropping to my knees, I wiped the cupboards, the chemical lemon smell of the spray choking me in the stifling bathroom. But still I scrubbed, ignoring the streak of blood on my cracked knuckles.

I imagined Mark waiting outside for me, sitting on the bed with his elbows braced on his knees. It was the way he sat whenever he was impatient, whenever this day rolled around, I found him sitting like that, his knee jumping.

The alarm on my phone beeped, making me jump, even though I'd been waiting for it. I left the cleaning supplies where they were and stood, blowing my hair off my sweaty forehead.

It's time.

I stepped towards the test. My pulse thumped in my throat and I crept slowly, as though I was approaching a predator – wary, prepared to strike. I reached for the stick of plastic and peered at the tiny screen.

One line.

My heart dropped like a stone. I held the test up, where the late morning sun was slanting yellow and oppressive through the window. Tilting it to the light, I searched for the merest hint of a second line, a shred of doubt. But the single line was a strong, unwavering, mocking pink. There was nothing beside it except barren white.

I fought the urge to scream, to throw the thing at the wall. Instead, I closed my eyes and thought of Mark. Sitting out there, waiting for news. I had to be strong. For him. To keep us going into the next month – the next cycle – that stretched endlessly ahead. The dread that seeped into me each time I had to take the test was eating away at me. After two years of trying, our lovemaking was beginning to lose its spontaneity.

I slid open the bathroom door and there he was on the end of the bed. His head snapped up, hope shining bright in his eyes.

'Sorry.' I dropped my head, squeezing my eyes closed. I knew if I had to endure the disappointment on his face, it would be my undoing.

'Don't say that… It's just one of those things.'

'Yeah, I know.' I sat beside him on the mattress. We didn't touch.

'We need to see that doctor.'

We'd been saying this for the last few months, but neither of us had made an appointment. We'd promised each other that this time, this month, would be the last time. That if today showed a negative, we'd see the doctor my sister recommended. She'd spent months trawling the net, reading reviews, making enquiries. This guy was supposed to be the best.

But I didn't want to go. Fertility tests would provide an answer, but what if the answer the was one we were both dreading? What if the last two years had been a waste of time? No one but my sister knew we were trying, but seeing a doctor was acknowledgement, an ominous step beyond the "We'll just try and see what happens" phase.

Silence sat like a weight between us.

'I might go for a drive,' I said softly.

Driving with all the windows down, hot air rushed into the Toyota. It tangled my hair, whipped under my clothes. I had no conscious destination in mind, but found myself heading out of town towards the beach. The way I always travelled whenever I needed to clear my head. Being the middle of summer, the beach would be packed with people but I had no intention of stepping out of the car.

The stereo blasted a playlist Mark had put together. Happy, carefree songs from the era when we'd met. Five years ago was like an eternal summer, a holiday, and every day was bliss. I smashed my palm against the power button. Silence was better. Silence suited my mood, and cast the music into the past where it belonged.

I wasn't sure if I could handle the doctor thing. I'd heard about fertility testing from a friend who'd been through it. The internal probing and the hormones, blood tests. Having sex on certain days of the month no matter what. God, talk about killing the romance.

'Damn it!' I screamed, pounding the steering wheel.

Why couldn't I get pregnant? In society it didn't seem so complicated; morons managed to get knocked-up every day. Had a few drinks, spread their legs, and bingo!

Mark and I had taken ages to decide we were ready... condoms and taking the pill religiously just in case there was an accident. An accident! I attempted a laugh, but it came out as more of a sob.

Taking a right, I drove along the road that headed to the beach. I could smell the salt from the ocean. Only ten more minutes, and I'd see the water through the windshield. I drove fast, taking the corners with ease. I pulled into the car park and turned off the engine. The damp sea air rushed through the lowered windows and I reclined my seat and closed my eyes. Guilt washed over me at leaving Mark alone when we should be dealing with this disappointment together. I always thought I was a strong person, but this... Seeing my sister and my gorgeous, pudgy niece just hammered home how much I wanted that life.

My sister and I, born only a year apart, were similar in so many ways, yet she'd fallen pregnant with Poppy without even trying. How could we be so different in that way? What was wrong with me?

I heard the tennis as soon as I stepped into the house. Nadal grunted his way towards the net, sweat flying. Mark sprawled on the couch, beer in hand. He smiled half-heartedly across the room at me.

'Who's winning?'

'Rafa. It's close though.'

I went to him, dropping onto the cushion beside him and burying my face into the soft, cotton sleeve of his t-shirt. 'Sorry I took off. I'm weak, I know.'

He chuckled, planting a kiss on my head. 'Come on, I get it.'

'Yeah, but to leave you here alone…'

'I've got beer.' He held out the bottle, and with a relieved smile I took it, taking a swig. There was the silver lining to getting my period each month.

We settled into silence, passing the bottle back and forth until it was empty, and then fetching more, sipping until the match was over, and Nadal was pumping his fist in glory.

I didn't particularly want to talk about what lay ahead of us, but the weight of it sat heavily on my shoulders. The only person I felt I could talk to about that, though, was my sister. Mark headed out to his shed, where he was building a cot for our baby. I'd seen the sketches but didn't understand much about types of wood and such things. Mark, as a builder, had taken time and an immense amount of pride to create the sketches and was now spending his spare time in the shed creating this masterpiece.

I heard the shed door squeak to a close and reached for my mobile, dialling my sister's number. 'Negative,' I blurted, cutting off her greeting.

'Oh, shit Em. I'm coming over.'

By the time I'd tidied up the kitchen and filled the kettle her car was screeching up the driveway. She let herself in the open screen door, navigating her way across the darkened lounge room. In the kitchen we embraced, and I let the tears go.

I tried not to cry with Mark, I tried to be strong. But I could cry with my sister. Bec wasn't the one I was letting down, and I knew she'd be there to comfort me the way a big sister could – without judgement, without pressure. That was why we'd chosen to tell her, and her only. Her no-bullshit personality and calm demeanour made her the logical choice.

She rubbed my back, her palm cool against my sweaty t-shirt. 'Don't panic,' she soothed. 'You'll get there.'

I pulled away, sniffing, and looked beyond her. 'Where's Poppy?'

She shrugged. 'She's home with Travis. Besides, she wouldn't want to see you so upset.'

'You don't have to leave my niece at home just because I can't give her a cousin.'

'Hey.' She stepped closer. 'Don't talk like that. Don't get bitter. I know it's hard, but you have to stay positive.'

'Two years, Bec,' I snapped, pulling mugs from the cupboard. I clattered around with the spoons, jar of instant coffee, slamming the fridge shut after snatching out the milk. 'I hate this. This day is torture. It's hell. Twenty-four times I've pissed on a stick and seen that result. I can't do this anymore.'

Bec boosted herself onto the kitchen bench beside me as I worked. 'Then it's time to see Dr Kemp.'

I sighed, handing her a mug. 'I know. I just have to psych myself up a bit.'

She took a sip and tried to hide her grimace. 'Hey, don't you have the exhibition opening tonight? That'll be good; it'll take your mind off things a bit. At least you can have a drink.'

I braced my elbows on the bench, tucking my chin in my hands. 'I don't think I can handle Patrick tonight. And I can't get pissed, being a work thing. But I really need a few to forget about today.'

'Don't worry about it. Get dressed up, keep busy. It'll be fine, Em.'

Slipping off my heels, I tiptoed up the hallway to the room at the end. Clutching the cold metal doorknob I took a sharp breath, then turned it. The door creaked open. A fresh paint smell lingered inside, and despite the heat of summer, it was cold, the air stale. My eyes roamed the blank white walls until they blurred, punctuated only by the grey curtains shut tight over the window.

I stifled a shudder. It was too empty in here.

Our empty room.

The white room.

Creeping to the cupboard, I peered inside at the neatly stacked plastic crates. *There. That's our baby. That could be all there will ever be.* Clothes, toys, books, sketches and paintings I'd done when I was still excited about the idea of a child.

It wasn't exciting anymore.

Dread. That's what I felt.

Lifting my black dress, I lowered myself carefully to my knees. The floorboards were hard and cold against my skin, such a contrast to the rest of the sweltering house. With this room closed up all the time, the sun could never penetrate it; we never came in here anymore.

Unfastening the lid of the top crate, I peered inside. On

top of a pile of clothes was a woollen hat with bunny ears stitched on the top. I'd found it at the market they held in town every month.

'Em, what are you doing in here?'

I spun. Mark, wrapped in a towel, stood frowning and dripping in the doorway. 'Are you okay?'

Sliding the hat back into the box, I struggled to my feet. I could smell his shower gel from where I lingered, with my heart thudding and heat climbing into my face. Why did I feel guilty?

Mark stepped over the threshold, and the clean, warm smell of him grew stronger. I slid my arms around his damp waist.

'So what time are we due at this thing?' he murmured, nuzzling his freshly-shaved chin into my neck.

'Patrick wants me at the gallery by six.'

'Shit, don't say his name,' he chuckled, holding me closer.

I grinned. 'Sorry.'

He drew back to look me in the eye. 'Come to bed with me. We've got time.'

'Honey…'

'Em, this room won't be empty forever. Don't give up on me.'

'Today's not the right day. I'm just about to get my–'

'Shhh,' he whispered, kissing my ear lobe.

I reached up to tousle his dark hair and smiled. A real, relaxed smile. It was rare that we made love on test day; it was such a depressing day. 'Okay.'

He tugged me by the hand down the hallway and we fell into our unmade bed, cotton sheets tangled with our legs, pillows flung to the floor as my dress was tossed to the armchair in the corner.

'I'm not ironing that again,' I told him as he settled between my thighs.

'And I won't mess up your makeup, darling,' he grinned.

I knew it would need a touch up; I knew we'd be sweaty after making love in our stifling bedroom. Briefly, I considered rolling over to flick on the electric fan but was soon lost in Mark's kisses, my skin zinging from his calloused fingertips, my hips opening as he pushed himself into me.

I don't care if we're late. I don't care if my dress is wrinkled. I don't care if my lipstick is smudged across my mouth.

Chapter 2

We arrived at the gallery only fifteen minutes late. Guests were due at any minute, and Patrick sauntered over when he saw me, looking as immaculate as always in his tailored suit, his hair parted to the side and slicked down.

'You're late.'

Mark bristled, pulling me up against him.

'Like I don't give you enough of my time?' I snapped.

Patrick laughed. 'Fair enough.'

I'd grown up alongside Patrick in this town. All through high school he had tormented me the way rich, arrogant kids did, making fun of my family's modest home and bragging about his own. Of course, it really was impressive. Three-storeys high and set up on a hill in The Grove, where the occupants could sneer down on the rest of us simple, middle-class folks. The high wall at the front even had a gargoyle perched on it, for God's sake.

His father, a frightening little man who thankfully didn't appear very often, had run the gallery his grandfather had created. Then he'd passed it onto Patrick to manage, while he kept himself occupied elsewhere. The family owned a substantial portion of the town, from the newspaper offices to several, ever-expanding housing estates. They owned the townhouse Mark and I lived in, too, although I tried not to dwell upon it.

Despite Patrick's snobbery, I tolerated him. I had handled the casual bullying while growing up; had shaken his hand from my breast in year ten with a stern reprimand, and I had accepted the arts assistant job when he'd offered it. I'd returned home from the city, broke and broken-hearted, with an arts degree and nothing else under my belt. I was desperate. But since working at the gallery, he'd paid me well and on time, and in return I worked hard. He was his usual dickhead self – it seemed he was never going to grow out of that – but he was my boss, nothing more.

Mark wasn't a local. We'd met five years ago when he was camping on the beach with his mates. It happened quickly, our relationship, and he'd dropped everything to live here with me. He didn't understand the local dynamics, and couldn't stand Patrick's arrogance. He hated that I worked at his family gallery; claimed Patrick *leered* at me. Frankly, I made a point not to notice.

'Patrick, mate, sorry we're late.' Mark shook his hand briefly with a tense smile.

Patrick's eyes swept down, taking in my wrinkled dress. 'No problem. Emily, I want you to meet our new employee.'

My head swivelled towards him. 'Our *what?*'

Patrick chuckled, sliding a hand into his pocket. 'I thought it was time to bring in some extra help. I can't run you ragged day after day forever, can I? You'll be starting a family at some point, no doubt.'

My stomach turned. *What does this mean? Does he know we're trying? Is he going to force me out?*

Beside me, I knew Mark was thinking the same thing. His hand has tightened in mine, to the point that my fingers were beginning to throb.

'Don't be silly,' I began, but my voice drifted away when a tall, blonde woman strutted out from the back office. Her dress – sleek, silver and strapless, barely covered perfectly proportioned curves. Her hair, a shimmering curtain the colour of sun-bleached sand, was trimmed evenly at shoulder length. Her tanned, long legs shone under the gallery lights, and her pouting lips were painted scarlet. It was as if she'd stepped right off a catwalk and into the small-town Alberton Art Gallery. She was so out of place, and seemed so unaffected by that fact, that my head actually began to hurt.

I glanced across at Mark, but his attention was fixed on this beautiful woman. Irritation prickled up my spine as the oxygen left my lungs. The room seemed to empty of air as the three of us stopped to watch her approach.

'Emily, this is who I was telling you about. Victoria. She's from Sydney, where she assisted at the Art Gallery of New South Wales. You won't have much to teach her.' Patrick's gaze travelled appreciatively from Victoria's strappy heels to her flawlessly painted face. 'I'm sure she'll catch on quickly to how I like things to be done around here.'

Victoria smiled, revealing straight, white teeth. 'Pat, you flatter me.' *Pat?* With her eyes on my husband, she said, 'Emily, it's nice to meet you. I've heard *great* things.'

'Yeah, hi,' I snapped, edging into her field of vision.

Finally she looked me in the eye and I flinched. Cats

eyes. Bright, vivid green… sly. Within her lurked the spirit of a predator.

'When did this happen?' I asked, turning to Patrick, unable to think of anything else to say.

'Quite quickly, as you can see,' Patrick answered, glancing across at Victoria. They shared a giggle. 'And you'll be happy to know, Emily, that Victoria has agreed to help the wait staff tonight, and will stay behind to clean up with me, so you can just relax and take the night off.' He beamed at me, expecting me to be happy, to beam right back, but all I could manage was a tight little smile.

'That's right, you can let your hair down,' Victoria chirped, and I looked at her, my fingers gripping my husband's, trying to quieten my mind – that was racing with hidden meaning and threats – before I said something regrettable and insulting. But was there something threatening about this woman or was I just intimidated by her beauty and confidence? In the end I chose not to answer, and stared at her instead, feeling the stoniness in my features and the peal of an alarm bell as she stared right on back, the smile dropping from her painted face.

'She's sleeping with him, Mark, I know it. There's definitely something going on. Who just walks in like that? Where did she even come from anyway? It's weird.' I waved the wine bottle in his direction. Despite the exhibition being a work function, the surprise of a stunning new employee – one who would probably be edging me out of my job sometime soon – had kept me reaching for the champagne all night, growing tipsier the more I watched Victoria swan around the gallery doing my job. Everyone had seemed charmed by her, freezing whenever she came close, smiling dreamily whenever she spoke to them. When I'd seen Patrick pat her arse, I'd swivelled to Mark to ask if he'd seen. He hadn't.

'Don't you think you've had enough to drink?' he asked now, clearly irritated. The clock was ticking towards midnight, and I'd been raving for the last hour about the future of my job.

'I'm not drunk,' I answered, passing him the bottle. 'I'm just pissed off. Today of all days, and I get news like this. I'm going to have a drink if I want, Mark.'

Mark grabbed the bottle and stood. 'You know what I think of your boss. He's a knob. But he made a point of saying this doesn't change anything for you.'

'There's not enough work for the two of us! And who do you think is going to get the most hours? Me? Or the one who looks like–'

'The competent one,' Mark interrupted.

'Competent at *what*? This is Patrick – *Pat* – we're talking about.'

Mark paced across the room, placing the almost-empty bottle on the kitchen bench and shutting off the lights. 'Come on, let's get to bed. I can't talk about this anymore.'

'I'm sorry, but I'm nervous. What if–'

'No what ifs, honey. Bed.'

We picked our way through the darkness towards the bedroom. I reached out like a blind woman, smoothing my hands over the sheets once I'd found them. I stretched my body across the mattress and sighed.

'Tomorrow's Sunday, isn't it?'

'See?' he laughed. 'If you don't know what day it is then

you've had enough to drink.'

I heaved another sigh. 'No, I have one more day to work out how to keep her from stealing my job.'

Mark groaned and flopped down beside me.

#

'Hey, Trav!'

'Marky Mark!'

I waited for the obligatory male shoulder slapping before giving my brother-in-law a kiss. He gave me a squeeze. 'Em, you still not drinking nowadays or can I get you a beer?'

'Nah, beer me. Thanks, Trav.'

Most Sundays the family got together at our parents' house for lunch – a barbecue or roast, depending on the weather.

I found Mum in the kitchen, putting salads together. Poppy sat beside her on the bench and I gravitated to her, kissing her blonde curls. She beamed up at me.

'Hello, precious. Look at you!' She wore a pastel-coloured tutu, dotted with sparkling sequins. Her sleeveless top brandished a shiny, pink unicorn. She grinned, seemingly pleased that I'd noticed her outfit.

Mum embraced me. 'How are you, darling?'

'Good,' I answered. 'Patrick's hired someone else at the gallery, though.'

Her head snapped towards me. 'Is your job protected?'

In spite of my own worry, I couldn't help but smile. 'He says it doesn't change anything.'

'So he's obviously not stepping back, or–'

'Nope, he's hired another assistant.'

Her brow creased. 'That's a bit of an insult, isn't it?'

'Yes!' I cried. 'Thank you. That's how I'm feeling. Mark says I'm being silly.'

'Well, it's early days. Don't worry yet.' She shook a bottle of balsamic dressing over a bowl. 'You know how I feel about that boy though. Wouldn't trust him as far as I could throw him.'

'I know, Ma.'

I twirled a finger through one of Poppy's curls. The sweet thing just sat, listening to Mum and me, toying with the lace of her skirt.

'And how have you been, princess?'

She smiled up at me. 'Good.'

'Where's your mum?'

'Bec's outside helping Pa fill up the pool. And Poppy's a bit quiet today, aren't you, love?'

The pool, as she called it, was a thin blue plastic pond, but was still a product of excitement for Poppy on hot days.

I held a hand to Poppy's forehead. She felt fine, and looked well enough, even though she did not seem her energetic self. 'I'm going out. Want to come, Pops?' When she nodded I lowered her to the floor.

'Hold her hand down the steps,' Mum called as we headed towards the back door. 'And tell Travis I'm still waiting for my beer!'

'Me too!' I called over my shoulder.

On the back patio, Mark and Travis sat reclined at the picnic table, beers in their hands, watching my dad and Bec wrestle with the pool. Poppy lifted her arms, and I carried her down the steps, tucking my chin into her warm weight.

She nestled into my chest and I swallowed hard, focusing my attention on my sister. Bec, her shorts riding up and her hair tied in a hurried topknot, bent over the blue plastic with my dad. They cackled together as the hose moved and sprayed water into their faces.

'Travis, where's that beer you promised?'

'Oh geez, sorry Em.' He nudged the esky with a thonged foot. 'Help yourself.'

I plopped down into a chair, still nursing Poppy. 'I suggest you get your arse up and hand me one. And your mother-in-law too, for that matter. She's waiting.'

'Shit.' That got him plodding back up the steps and into the house, carrying a couple of fresh stubbies. I sipped from my own, smiling across at Mark. But he wasn't looking at me; his soft gaze was on Poppy. I watched him watching us, my free hand rubbing her back in slow circles, her cheek pressed against me as she relaxed into sleepiness.

I swallowed past the bitter taste in my mouth; it wasn't from the beer. What if I couldn't give him this? What if it never happened for us? I wanted to see that look on his face as he gazed at our own child.

Closing my eyes, I pressed my lips into Poppy's soft warm skin. She smelled of sunscreen and sunshine. And my heart hurt.

'Can you take her? I'm going to help Dad and Bec with the pool.' I handed a sleepy Poppy to Mark, turning away as he carefully bundled her up in his arms.

'Hi, love!' Dad called as I approached. He squinted up at me from where he sat on the grass, patching a hole in the flimsy plastic with duct tape. 'Come here and give me a kiss.'

I knelt beside him and pecked his cheek. He wrestled

me into a rough hug, his hairy arms damp from the pool. As I settled beside him with a smile, my abdomen cramped. My period was coming, and there was nothing I could do to stop it.

'How's work?'

I filled him in on the new employee. Dad didn't react too much, as expected, and Bec settled my anxiety simply by joining us on the grass. Dad and Bec were the calm ones, looking at the bright side and believing the best of people.

'You know it's just a job, though, love?' Dad said finally.

'It's *my* job, Dad, and I've worked hard. Patrick doesn't do that much, just swans about in his shiny shoes.'

Bec laughed. 'He wore shiny shoes in primary school. He's such a dickhead.'

When my stomach cramped again, I pressed a palm against it. Bec met my eyes, her smile fading.

'Are we eating or paddling first?' she asked Dad.

'Ask your mother,' he replied, fiddling with the tape. 'You know who runs the show around here.'

An hour later, we watched Dad and Poppy splash in the plastic pool, floppy hats shading them from the afternoon sun. I reclined in my seat, propping my bare feet on the tabletop, dodging the remains of our barbeque lunch. I felt drowsy from the beer and the sun, and closed my eyes, listening to the rest of my family chattering around me.

I tried not to think about work or babies or anything else. Bec was right; I couldn't let myself get bitter. I didn't want to get sucked into any office bitchiness either. I'd never been that type of girl. I had to focus on staying relaxed, creating a loving environment with Mark. I hadn't given in and researched anything – best sex positions, diets, and whatever else – because I knew it would shove us out of that "Let's see what happens" phase. It turned out the clock managed to do that all by itself. I had to focus on keeping my attitude positive.

Fight the clock.

The storm rolled in just before midnight.

I lay facing the window, knees tucked up, arms wrapped across my cramping stomach. Mark spooned me from behind as we lay in the dark, listening to the wind buffeting the house. The curtains gusted into the room, but neither of us bothered to get up and shut the window, even when the mist of rain touched my skin. It pounded down outside, against the corrugated iron roof, against the driveway. Thunder churned and crashed, lightning lit up the room with eerie blue-white light.

The symbolism wasn't lost on me; the weather matched my mood perfectly.

Sunday nights after our family lunches were always fairly quiet between Mark and me, and tonight was no exception. As each month ticked by, the weight of our childless future grew a little heavier. I knew we had to take the next step. I turned over to face Mark. His face was illuminated briefly by a flash of lightning. 'Should I call the doctor?' I asked, raising my voice over the weather.

He propped himself up on an elbow. 'Maybe it's time, honey.' He bent down and kissed me on the tip of my nose.

'You're always quiet after we see Poppy.'

After a moment's silence, he chuckled, 'She's such a cute little kid. It hurts.'

I didn't say anything else, turning back towards the window and tucking my pillow under my head. Mark nestled down behind me, resting an arm across my hip.

We lay still and listened to the storm, our bodies joined and warm.

Chapter 3

Monday morning I promised to make an effort, and dress with extra care. But standing naked in the walk-in closet, all my choices filled me with despair. I kept picturing Victoria slinking around in her silky sliver of a dress and knew there was absolutely nothing I could do. I couldn't compete with her in the looks department, I just had to go to the gallery and do my job.

I settled on a green dress with loose sleeves to hide my plump arms. Sucking my tummy in, I posed in front of the mirror, sighing. It would have to do. I carefully applied makeup, smudging the eyeliner a little to emphasise my best feature. Strapping on my sandals, I let myself out of the house, hoping that by arriving early and working my arse off I would make it clear I wasn't planning on going anywhere.

Opening the gallery door, I heard a flirtatious giggle and my stomach dropped. *She's already here.*

'Morning!' I sang, hating the fake joviality in my voice.

In the office, Victoria perched on the edge of my desk, chatting to Patrick. Her long legs were crossed but she was wearing pants this time, at least. She sipped from a mug, *my mug*, as Patrick talked, and it appeared she was listening carefully.

'Hi Emily!' she chirped as I locked my bag in the filing cabinet. At my desk, I manoeuvred my chair around her and sat, flicking on my computer. There, beside the monitor, two photos. The first showed Victoria and a child, smiling sweetly into the camera. And in the second one the same child had a face smeared with ice cream.

'Oh,' I murmured, turning to Patrick. 'Victoria and I are sharing a desk?'

'Well, you are sharing a job, so yes.' He smirked, straightening his shirt collar.

'Can I talk to you for a minute?' I gestured to the kitchen, throwing a polite smile in Victoria's direction as I left the room.

Easing the kitchen door shut, I turned to Patrick. 'I didn't get a chance to ask you the other night, Patrick, but what the hell is going on?'

He leant against the counter and crossed his arms. 'What?'

'With her.' I lifted my chin in the direction of the office. 'Since when do we need another employee? I'm managing okay, aren't I?'

Patrick nodded. 'Well, sure you are, honey–'

'Don't call me honey.'

'Sorry. Yes, you are managing.' He sighed. 'But we want to expand the gallery. We've been sitting pretty for years but nothing is really changing. I want more exhibitions, I want to invite new artists into our space. I can't rely on you to hold down the fort on your own, with me stepping out, going to meetings. Victoria will add a freshness to the gallery, and she's experienced.' He grinned. 'I think it'll be great.'

I took a step towards him. 'Tell me honestly,' I said, voice low. 'Are you planning to get rid of me?'

He blew out a long breath, cheeks puffing out. 'Of course not. You don't have to feel insecure, just ride with it. We'll work out hours as we go along.'

'She's already got photos on the desk, Patrick.'

He frowned. 'Which means she feels comfortable here. Can't you be a little nicer?'

My heart rate kicked up a notch. 'I'm just a little blindsided here.'

'I've been talking about expanding the gallery for months.'

'Well, in my defence, you do talk a lot of bullshit, Patrick.'

He threw his head back and laughed. 'Right, so tell me how you really feel! Well, she's here, I've hired her, so you two will have to get along.'

I smirked. 'Sure you're not after a cat fight? Because you're not going to get one. Not my style.'

He nodded. 'Message received. Now get to work.'

I made my way out of the kitchen, receiving a tap to my arse as I passed him. I spun around with a glare.

He cleared his throat. 'Sorry.'

I sat at my desk again and logged in. The computer sprang to life, revealing a new desktop picture. Victoria holding an armful of kittens, head back, laughing with joy. *She's here for five minutes and already fucks with my computer?* I managed to take a slow, steady breath without drawing attention to myself. Ignoring the new background, I opened up the gallery calendar, checking the list of tasks I had to do today.

'Right,' I called through the doorway to Patrick. 'I'm going to call Ben Gardner to pick up the work that didn't sell. Did you want to chat to him when–'

'Oh, I've done that,' Victoria interrupted. I turned to where she was standing by the file cabinets. She shrugged and smiled. 'We thought I should get to know the local artists.'

'Okay,' I replied, spinning away from her. I eyed Patrick in his office, left foot propped on his desk as he shined his shoe. 'Okay then,' I murmured. 'I'll pay these bills.'

Victoria cleared her throat. 'I've done those too. Patrick was teaching me the system, and–'

'I understand,' I snapped, but I didn't, not really. Where had this woman come from?

I watched as she collected a stack of paper from the printer and sauntered into Patrick's office. He smiled up at her, eyes glittering. I sat at our shared desk – it wasn't just mine anymore – and felt small and insignificant.

As soon as I pulled into the garage and turned off the engine, I burst into tears. I felt soiled after a day in Victoria's company, exhausted and empty. Too aware of the blood pulsing out of me, of the call I had to make. I was so hot, my clothes had glued themselves to my skin; I'd zoomed home frantically, needing to get the hell out of there, and forgotten to turn on the air conditioner or wind down a window.

Sitting in the dark garage, I took a shaky breath, willing myself to calm down. I thought of Mark probably already inside, waiting for me to come home. I thought of the baby we couldn't have, of my period that showed up every month to mock me.

Wiping my face, I dialled my GP's office and made an appointment for the following afternoon. Step one, making the appointment. Step two, admitting my failure… that wouldn't be so easy.

Inside the house, a blast of coolness from the air con greeted me. I called out for Mark but with no reply, headed to the shower. In clean PJs, hair washed, I finally felt cleansed of my day. Mark was on the couch with two icy beers on the coffee table in front of him. He patted the couch cushion and I fell down beside him. He hadn't showered since work and I inhaled the sawdust and sweat, kissing the salty skin of his shoulder. I told him I called the doctor and he nodded, passing me a stubby. I didn't bother telling him the rest – about the new atmosphere in the office and Victoria attacking my to-do list. The last thing I needed was for him to tell me I was overreacting. Plus, I didn't want to think about it anymore.

So I sat, and I drank.

I woke in the morning resolved to make more of an effort at work, to get to know Victoria a little bit. If she was going to be a permanent fixture at the gallery, or even a semi-permanent one, then it'd be best if we could be friends.

She's not the kind of person I would be friends with, but I can do this. I stared at my reflection, pulling my skirt into place. *This is my job. I need to take the initiative here.*

I surged through the morning beaming like a ray of sunshine, making Victoria coffee (not in my mug) and as the morning headed towards the noon hour, I braced myself and asked her for lunch.

She spun to me, and those eyes narrowed with suspicion. Then she grinned, flashing perfect teeth. 'Great!'

We crossed the street to Cleo's Café, waiting for a gap in traffic and making a dash for it. Inside, the café was busy, but I led the way to an empty table right up the back. Locals I recognised turned to stare at Victoria as we passed, and she tossed her hair and smirked at them, seemingly loving the attention. Once we sat, hooking our bags on the backs of our chairs, an awkward silence fell. I cleared my throat, smiling at her across the table.

'So, Victoria, tell me about you. What brings you to Alberton?'

She smoothed a palm over her hair and pressed her lips together. Suddenly she seemed nervous, or unsure how to answer the question. 'Well, you see–'

The waitress bustled over, slapping two menus on the table. 'Hi, Em, how are you, hon?'

I glanced up. 'Hi, Cleo. I'm good.' Bec's friend smiled, her dark eyes darting over to Victoria. 'This is Victoria,' I obliged. 'She's new at the gallery.'

'Really?' Cleo propped a hand on her hip and turned to Victoria. 'I'm Cleo, a friend of Em's sister.'

Victoria smiled politely, lips thin, looking uncomfortable. 'Nice to meet you.'

Cleo laughed. 'We're like family round here, so welcome, hey? Just holler when you're ready to order.' She spun on her heel, weaving expertly around the packed tables and heading back behind the counter.

We both ordered chicken and sweet potato salads. I speared a piece of avocado and looked her in the eye. 'You started to tell me why you moved to Alberton?'

She finished chewing before she answered. 'I used to live in Melbourne when I was a kid. Before I moved to Sydney. And I love the beach, so coming back this way was a logical choice.' She paused, sipping her water. 'Change of scenery, you know.'

'And the girl in the pictures, is she your daughter?'

A tight nod. 'Lily.'

'She's beautiful. How's she settling in?'

She dropped her fork and swiped at her napkin, rubbing at her fingers. 'She's still with my mum. I wanted to get things organised before she comes.'

I watched her wiping her hands and swallowed. 'You must miss her.'

'Of course,' she replied, a little tersely. She finally looked up and forced herself to smile, but the smile was as false as they came. 'It's been hard, but things will be okay soon. Now, enough about me. What about you and that lovely husband of yours?'

And just like that, her vulnerability was gone, and the predator was back. She tugged at her lower lip with her teeth and held my gaze. Daring me to react? I ate a piece of chicken, breathing deeply. I'd seen her sadness, her doubts, her hands shaking. She wasn't happy, and as nasty as it felt, that made me feel slightly better about my own little life, even if Mark and I couldn't make a baby. I wasn't going to be fooled by this woman who seemed secure, but wasn't.

'Mark and I have been married for four years. I've been at the gallery with Patrick for about nine years now.'

'Wow, that's a while. And do you have kids?'

'No,' I answered, aware that I had snapped a little, but she didn't seem to notice.

'You should. They're precious. They bring so much love into your life. There's no other love like it. And you two would make a beautiful child.' Her eyes glittered and she bared her teeth in a smile that looked more like a snarl.

Narrowing my eyes, I pushed away my salad. I'd lost count of the amount of times I'd heard a similar comment from people I didn't know very well, and it staggered me. Why did people think they had the right to say such things? How did they think it was any of their business? It was different if a relative or a close friend made such a statement – although I still found it inappropriate and insulting – but I didn't know this woman.

I nudged my chair back and crossed my ankles. 'Mark and I are doing just fine, thanks very much.'

Victoria's mouth opened. Her eyes darted to the left, the right, and then settled on me. 'I crossed a line? Sorry.'

But she didn't look sorry. Instead she stared at me hard, eyebrows slightly raised, lips upturned in a half-smile, and waited for my response.

'You know what?' I answered finally, keeping my voice low. 'It's cool. I'm used to people asking me when we're having kids. But it's really no one's business.'

She grinned, those white teeth flashing again, and took a tiny sip of water with measured coolness. 'You're right. It's a personal thing.'

'Exactly, I mean, you should understand since you're separated from your daughter at the moment, and I have no right to ask you *why*.'

Her water glass thumped against the table top and I felt a rush of bitter satisfaction. I stopped there, unused to bitchiness, and not wanting to enrage this unpredictable woman. When she hadn't answered a couple of minutes later, I threw my crumpled napkin onto my half-eaten salad.

'We should get going, don't you think?' I stood, berating myself for getting sucked in to her scheming. After telling myself I was going to be nice, that I wasn't going to bite, I hadn't lasted long at all.

Dr Curtis ushered me into his office. As usual his desk was a mess, cluttered with piles of folders, half-opened mail and pamphlets. Medical posters papered the walls and a huge out of date scale dominated the corner of the room. I perched on one of the squeaky leather chairs, my heart thudding. I'd never spoken to Dr Curtis about anything as personal as this before.

'Emily, it's been a long time. How are you going?'

I opened my mouth, but all that came out was a pathetic sob. Heat flooded to my face and I hung my head, mortified.

'Oh, Emily, it's okay.' Dr Curtis scooted over to me in his chair, brandishing a box of tissues. His bald head shone under his desk lamp and he smiled kindly in the warm light. 'Whatever you tell me will be kept in confidence, you know that.' He placed a soft palm on my arm for a moment and waited.

'I can't get pregnant,' I whispered.

'I see. And how long have you and Mark been trying?'

'Two years.' I looked up at him, swiping at my eyes. 'That's bad, isn't it?'

He grimaced. 'After twelve months I'd encourage you to see a fertility specialist.'

I nodded. 'Yeah, so, it's bad.'

Dr Curtis sat back in his seat with a sigh. 'Look, everyone is different and it's hard to tell you what you should do, which is why I think a specialist is the way to go.'

'And what will they do?'

'They will run some tests, talk to you about your menstrual cycle and your lifestyle, and that type of thing.'

'When should I go?'

'Dr Kemp comes here every month from the city. So if I write you a referral today, we can make an appointment for as soon as possible. First though, you'll need to have a pelvic ultrasound, and we'll get you a blood test as well to check out your hormone levels. He would get you to do that anyway, so we can save some time by doing that now.' He paused. 'And try not to worry, Emily. So many couples have difficulties and go on to have perfectly healthy babies.'

I stirred the pasta sauce and sprinkled in some chopped basil. I'd showered after returning from the doctor's and felt fresh again, like I'd washed off the day. My damp hair was curling in the steamy air and I opened the back door to let in the breeze.

Tossing spaghetti in the pot of boiling water on the other burner, I took a huge swig from my wine glass. I missed drinking during the month, and made up for it – probably a bit too eagerly – while I had my period. Draining my glass, I poured another.

'Thirsty?'

I spun, smiling at Mark. 'You're late.'

'Yep. But I was thinking of you the whole time.'

Laughing, I sank into his arms. He stunk of sweat and sawdust, my lips collecting grit from his neck. 'Hungry? I'm making spaghetti.'

'Yeah, of course. Smells good.' He pressed his lips on to the top of my head. 'So, did you see Dr Curtis?'

'He's writing me a referral.'

Mark blew out a breath, lifting my hair. 'Well done you. I'm proud of you, honey.'

I pulled back, patting his chest. The cooking had been good, keeping my mind occupied. But with Mark's question, the emotion of the afternoon's appointment was coming back. 'Why don't you go shower and I'll take care of this.'

I checked my pots, set out two bowls, cutlery, serviettes and a bowl of parmesan. I poured a glass of wine for Mark and by the time he'd joined me in the kitchen, dinner was ready and music was playing. While we ate, he reached over the table and entwined his fingers through mine. We didn't need to rehash our day, I realised, twirling my spaghetti.

I clenched his fingers tighter.

#

'Up on the table, Emily.'

Pressing my knees together, I swivelled myself on to the table and yanked the blue sheet over my legs. The dim room glowed with monitors in an attempt to be relaxing, possibly, but I shuddered in the cool hospital air. The plastic-covered pillow squeaked under my neck as I lay back, my hands balled into fists against my chest.

'Relax, sweetie, it's okay. It's not going to hurt.' The nurse smiled and her eyes crinkled. She had a motherly air, and it worked. I took a breath and loosened my muscles. I didn't look, but I heard the squirt of lubricant and then the object was pushing into me. *Breathe.* Another deep breath when I felt the wand move, and I closed my eyes. She was right. It didn't hurt. But I wanted this over. I wanted to run.

'What can you see?'

'It's not really my place tell you…'

'Please tell me something,' I urged as she moved the wand again, stretching me out to the side. I grimaced.

'Well, everything looks pretty good, Emily.'

'Really?' My head swivelled to the screen, but there were grey shadows and nothing more.

'No sign of cysts on the ovaries, which is good, and your uterus looks fine.' She withdrew the wand and passed me a handful of tissues. 'Of course, the doctor will tell you more, but I couldn't see anything for you to be alarmed about.'

I sighed. 'That's great. Thank you.'

She smiled her eye-crinkling smile. 'I'll leave you to get dressed. Good luck, darling.'

'Thanks.'

'How'd it go?'

Mark poked his head through the garage door as soon as I'd turned off the ignition. Bare-chested, he held a wooden spoon aloft, his hair dishevelled.

'What have you been doing?' I laughed, reaching for the spoon.

'Making dinner,' he grinned. 'I haven't had a chance to shower; I wanted to have the food ready.'

'You're a sweetheart.'

'So?' he prompted, hooking my bag over his shoulder and walking us into the house. 'How did it go? What did the doctor say?'

'It was a nurse, and she couldn't tell me heaps but she said there's nothing noticeable for me to worry about.'

Mark sighed. 'That's so good, honey. Did it hurt?'

I shook my head. 'Nah. I do want to clean up though.'

He nodded. 'Go ahead. I'll serve up.'

'It smells good,' I called, shutting myself in the bathroom. I turned on the tap and washed my hands, scrubbing away the hospital smell. Then stripping off my clothes, I tossed them over the edge of the bath, and reached into the cupboard for a washcloth. A bottle of yellow liquid caught my eye and I fished it out. It was a full bottle of baby shampoo. Bec must have left it there for some reason, but Poppy didn't use that shampoo, she used the bottle with the princesses on it. Frowning, I tucked it back into the cupboard and closed the door.

I stepped into the shower to rinse off before dinner.

Chapter 4

'Why am I so nervous?' Reapplying my lipstick. Rubbing it off.

'I'm not sure,' Bec answered from where she sat cross-legged on my bed. 'You're not going on a date, this is a colleague. And you have the upper hand. You've been there longer.'

'You don't understand.' I boosted my boobs, shook my top into place. 'You haven't seen her.'

'What does that mean?'

'It means she has this scary, supermodel thing going on.'

Bec scooped out a handful of peanuts from the bowl beside her. 'And why is that scary?'

'It just is. You'll see.'

'Cleo said she seems shy.' She crunched her nuts, eyeing me with what looked like amusement.

'You're making fun of me.'

I turned back to the mirror and squinted at my reflection. Sheer black top with a bit of sparkle, tight jeans that weren't too tight, and strappy sandals. I looked okay. But no matter how hard I tried, I couldn't tame the small frizzy hairs escaping my ponytail.

'I've just never seen you go to this much trouble before.' Bec stood, dusting her palms. 'We better go.'

We pulled up outside Cleo's Café ten minutes later and Bec switched off the ignition. Through the windows, the café was half full, mostly after-work drinkers and diners. I couldn't spot Victoria anywhere.

'Right, which one is she?'

'I don't think she's here yet.' I unclipped my seat belt. 'Which is good, because we can settle in first.'

Bec chuckled as she climbed out of the car. We waved to Cleo as we headed into the café and found two free seats at the bar. I ordered a Coke, scanning the room, smiling at familiar faces and breathing a sigh of relief when I confirmed Victoria wasn't here yet. Sipping my drink, I ushered Cleo over and asked about a table.

'Don't stress. I'm off in a second, so I'm going to sit with you guys. I'll get us a table.' She untied her apron as she spoke and flung it over the counter. 'You look great, by the way. So dressed up.'

I forced a smile. 'Yeah, I'm not sure why.'

Beside me, Bec snorted. 'You haven't seen Victoria yet, have you Cleo? I'm dying to meet her.'

Cleo shook her head. 'It's weird that Patrick hired someone else. You two were managing the gallery just fine, weren't you?'

I shrugged. 'I thought so, yeah.'

She returned my shrug. 'Well, who knows what goes through that guy's head. Might have some grand plans for an art festival or something.' She took off, bustling through the crowd. Soon enough, she was calling us over to a cleared table. We sat at the same time a waitress brought over a jug of water and three glasses.

'Not drinking tonight, C?' Bec asked, splashing water into the cups.

'Well,' Cleo cleared her throat. 'I have a good reason for it.' She squirmed in her seat and on an instinctive level I knew what was coming. I drew in a slow silent breath through my teeth. 'I'm pregnant,' Cleo finished, her face glowing pink.

Under the table, Bec clutched at my hand, digging in her nails. To Cleo, she grinned and reached over with her other hand. 'That's fabulous, C. Congratulations!'

I joined in, leaning over to peck her on the cheek. My stomach sucked against my spine, my heart felt like it was being squeezed by an iron fist. A hot flush washed up from my belly, climbing my throat. Fighting to stay calm, I listened to Cleo's voice hammering out the details along with my thumping pulse. I waited for Victoria to show up, to turn heads as she breezed in looking amazing, to strengthen my feelings of inadequacy. *God, what's wrong with me?* I hated myself in that moment, for not being as happy for Cleo as I should have been, for feeling threatened by a colleague who happened to be beautiful. How ridiculous. I had a loving husband at home, and a sister who was holding my hand to keep me anchored.

I was lucky.

I forced myself to ask Cleo questions, to nod eagerly as I listened. We ordered appetisers, and I scooped cheese onto crackers and sipped my drink as the girls talked about childbirth. I could feel the weight of Bec's stare as she checked on me every few seconds, and I involved myself in the conversation as much as I could, making all the appropriate faces and noises. I couldn't add anything of course, so mostly listened, and when the subject eventually settled, I blew out a long breath. It was then I realised that Victoria still hadn't shown up. Checking my phone, I whispered to Bec that it was nearing nine thirty and Victoria was an hour and a half late.

'Safe to assume she's not coming then?'

I shrugged. 'Suppose not. Want to head off?'

We said our goodbyes and Bec dropped me off home. With the engine idling, she reached over for a hug. 'Are you okay? You know, about Cleo's announcement?'

'I'm okay.' I unbuckled my seat belt. 'We're at the age where this is happening more and more and I'm going to have to get used to it.'

'I'm sorry I didn't change the subject earlier, but it would've been weird if I–'

'It's okay.' I hugged her again, tighter this time. 'I'm okay. And we can't say I didn't try to make nice with Victoria either. So, you know, tonight wasn't how we planned it, but it's okay. I've got a gorgeous man waiting inside for me.'

We both turned to look at the house. The lounge room window was glowing yellow around the curtains. Mark was still up.

I climbed out of the car and blew Bec a kiss, then ran up the path to the front door.

#

The afternoon sweltered, the air con not doing much

to cool down the house. In the lounge room, Mum and I sprawled on the couch, bare legs sticking to the leather. The curtains were shut to the orange sun, the TV glowing with its blue tennis court. On the screen, Rafa and Roger walked out to rapturous applause.

'I thought ice water would be good too.' Mark set down a tray of cold beers, a water jug and glasses. Condensation dripped from the brown bottles.

'You're a handy husband, aren't you, darling?' Mum beamed, reaching for a beer.

'Speaking of husbands, where's Dad?' I asked, pouring myself some water.

Mum took a swig and sighed. 'Guess where? At Bunnings again. He's obsessed. He has so many little projects going on. You should see the garage; can barely fit the bloody car in.'

'Retirement suits him,' Mark grinned. 'Oh, hey, it's starting.'

'So is Dad coming over?' I asked as the crowd on screen roared.

'He'll be along once he's ready.'

We turned to the TV and absorbed ourselves in the match, laughing at Mum's comments about Roger's perfectly shaped legs. Bec, Travis and Poppy had a birthday party to attend, so Mum had forgone Sunday lunch plans and come to our place instead. Every year we watched the Australian Open final together as we all loved tennis and had played at the club growing up. Mum had encouraged the sport based on her love for it; Bec was never very good at it, but I had entered local tournaments and done okay. Once I'd finished high school though, I'd put the racquet down and hadn't picked it up since.

After the first set, Dad still hadn't arrived, and Mark went to replenish the drinks and fetch some snacks from the kitchen. We were wilting in the steamy afternoon, shifting positions to find cool patches of couch.

'So, can I ask you something, honey?' Mum asked softly, looking sidelong at me.

'Hmmm? Is it about Roger again?'

She chuckled. 'No. I noticed when I went to the loo earlier that you still haven't done anything with that spare room.'

I glanced at her. 'So?'

'Just wondering if you've got plans for it?' Her voice had lowered further and her eyes gleamed with intensity.

So this was it. Mum had never mentioned us having kids before; she preferred to mind her own business when it came to private things. But I could see where this conversation was heading.

'Do you have something in mind?' I asked carefully.

'Well,' she answered slowly, toying with a golden earring, 'it might make a nice bub's room if you and Mark were heading that way. It's close to your bedroom, and the bathroom, and you could decorate it nice. I could help.'

I swallowed past the lump in my throat. This was the time to tell her, to tell her about our struggles, our appointments, to get her support. But Mark and I had promised. I couldn't.

'Thanks for the input, Mum.' I put down my empty glass on the coffee table. 'We're not sure what we're using the room for.'

'Okay.' She patted my knee, and leaned in close as Mark's footsteps neared the lounge room. 'If you ever want to talk, you know you can tell me anything.' She held my gaze with hers, and nodded once.

My heart rate sped up. Had Bec said something to her? Had someone seen me at the hospital and reported back? Did she *sense* something in that instinctive, maternal way that supposedly made all mothers psychics? I knew Mark wouldn't have told her anything, and surely Bec wouldn't have either.

I tried to put Mum's comments out of my mind and watch the tennis, but it was difficult. In my head, I was in that empty white room down the hall, sorting through crates of baby clothes and hanging them in the wardrobe.

'Of course I didn't say anything.'

Mark propped himself on an elbow, his forehead creased in annoyance. We were both sweaty after sex, and I kicked the sticky sheet away from my legs.

'Don't be annoyed. I knew you wouldn't have.'

'Then why bloody ask?' He turned his back and sipped from a glass of water by the bed.

'I'm just telling you what she said,' I snapped back, picking up my t-shirt and pulling it over my head.

'I knew this would happen,' he murmured.

'What?'

'Your family is so close, they tell each other everything. Why did we think Bec would be able to keep this a secret?'

I reached over and pressed my palm against his back, felt his heart thumping underneath. 'We don't know, okay? Mum might just be fishing for information. She probably doesn't know anything.'

Mark sighed, turned to face me. 'I don't want everyone to

know. But I shouldn't be surprised, I guess. I've never known a family so close.'

I nodded, smiled. His family was so different. He didn't know his dad, and he was an only child. His mother moved to Tasmania with her new partner several years ago and contacted him on birthdays and Christmas, and that was about it. His aunt Marilyn visited now and then, and the relationship was friendly enough, but unemotional. He had fit into my family seamlessly, I'd thought, and loved them so much. But it wasn't the type of family life he understood.

'Come on, let's go to sleep.' I tugged at his hand, but he grimaced, pulled away.

'You know, I might go and work for a while, if that's okay. I'm not sleepy just yet.'

I watched him dress, resting back against the pillows. I listened to the door click shut, the shed door creak open. I listened for the sounds of his woodworking, but the only sound was from the fan propped in the corner of the bedroom, whirring and stirring dust.

Chapter 5

Monday morning, Victoria met me at the gallery door.

'I'm so sorry about Friday night. I completely forgot, and then when I realised it was too late and I didn't have your number, and…' Her hands fluttered around her throat as she talked, but despite this anxious gesture, she appeared as flawless as usual. Her hair was tied up in a knot, sides smooth without a strand out of place. Her makeup was thick but flattering; eyes outlined expertly and lipstick perfect. I couldn't have managed that if I'd spent hours in front of the mirror.

'It's okay, Victoria.' I shrugged, and she sighed deeply.

'We should reschedule. I really want to meet your sister, and she can bring her adorable daughter along too.'

'Poppy?' I frowned. 'How do you know about Poppy?'

Her lips thinned, those cat-like eyes hardened, and I felt the storm clouds roll in. 'Patrick,' she said flatly. 'Patrick has mentioned her. He told me how he's known your family a long time.'

I shifted my bag to my other shoulder. Awkwardness had

descended and I wasn't sure why. Victoria was blocking me from entering the gallery properly, and I took a step forward to try to encourage her to let me in. She didn't move.

'Well, Patrick doesn't know my family, really. Just Bec and me. We went to school together.'

'That's what I meant.' She snapped the words, but she flashed a dazzling smile. 'Anyway. We'll reschedule, hey? Can I get you a coffee?'

'Sure. Thanks.'

She stalked away, posture rigid, heels clacking on the tiles. Why did I feel so uncomfortable? I couldn't put my finger on it. I followed her slowly and put away my bag. Patrick's office was empty, and I couldn't be bothered asking where he was. No doubt Victoria would know exactly what was going on; I still had my suspicions that they were sleeping together, and that maybe for some reason their pillow talk included discussing my niece. Irritation sparked in my chest.

Reschedule we would, and Bec, in her calm, no-bullshit manner, would tell me exactly what the deal was with Victoria, and whether it was valid for me to feel so threatened.

#

I held out a towel and Bec lifted a slippery Poppy from the bath and into my arms. I wrapped her up in it, dampness leaching into my clothes but I didn't care. It was the mundane, everyday things I was looking forward to most – the messy meals, the same bedtime story over and over, bath time with the floaty toys and fine hair shampooed into spikes.

'Okay, possum, here we go.' I set Poppy down and Bec

and I wrestled her into her nightie. I combed her wet hair, making faces at her in the mirror to make her laugh. When Bec left me and went to serve up the spaghetti for our dinner, I sat beside Poppy on her bed and kissed her forehead. Her bedroom was decked out in a princess theme; I'd been in here hundreds of times but I never got tired of it. There was a castle Bec had painstakingly stencilled on one wall, complete with turrets and a moat. Fairy lights were strung across the ceiling, a shag rug dyed in different shades of pink covered the old boards on the floor, and ballerinas, fairies and other pretty dolls were lined up along the shelves and the side of the bed. A rack of colourful tutus, tiaras and fairy wings sat in one corner. A pale pink canopy of floaty tulle covered her bed.

'Will you be here in the morning?' Poppy whispered, her eyelids heavy.

'No, I'll be at my house. But how about I visit again tomorrow?'

She smiled, nodding drowsily.

I flicked on the rainbow night light beside the bed, smoothed the sheet across her tiny body, and tiptoed out of the room. Outside, in the hallway, I leaned against the wall and drew in a long breath.

She never failed to drive a stake through my heart.

The smell of spaghetti sauce drew me to the kitchen, where Bec was passing bowls over the serving bench to Travis and Mark. Bec and Travis had decorated the old farmhouse beautifully; the kitchen had the original combustion stove and hardwood floors, and since the bones of the house were good, they didn't have to do much structurally. The kitchen had been modernised though, with a serving bench inserted to open up the wall between the kitchen and dining room. Bec had added stainless steel appliances, as she loved to cook and spend time in the kitchen. Travis had known the previous owner, and builder, of the house, so he was passionate about respecting the building.

We ate on the back veranda, where the heat of the day had finally simmered down to a manageable level. A warm breeze stirred around our bare feet, lifting fine dust from the wooden boards. Crickets chirped from unseen places, and birds swooped from clear skies to collect bugs in their beaks. The surrounding paddocks glowed gold under the lowering sun, their grasses waving gently in the wind. The whole scene was idyllic, peaceful. Bec and Travis were lucky to snag this place, this gorgeous patch of land. It was the perfect place to raise a family.

Once Mark and Travis were engaged in an animated conversation about something or other, I leaned close to Bec and whispered, 'Have you said anything to Mum?'

She frowned. 'About what?'

'She wanted to know what we were going to use the spare room for.'

Bec leaned back in her chair. 'Oh. No, of course not. She's probably just fishing for information.'

'That's exactly what I said.' I lifted my chin in Mark's direction, who was still chatting to Travis. 'That's not like her though.'

Bec shrugged, indifferent. And just like that, the conversation was over. We joined in with Mark and Travis, who had moved on to discussing the tennis final. As the sun sank lower, my mind cleared, and the last of the heat dissolved. I rubbed my cooling arms, batting at the buzz of a mosquito. It was time to move indoors, or time to head home. I caught Mark's eye. He looked weary. Time to go home then.

As we waved and backed out the long gravel driveway, I asked Mark if he was okay.

'Just nervous about tomorrow,' he said. And just like that, my peace was shattered. Tomorrow. Our appointment with the fertility doctor. I returned to reality with a crash, as behind us through the windscreen, Bec and Travis's exquisite little farmhouse disappeared from view.

#

We crossed the hospital parking lot, hands sealed to each other's with sweat. We followed the signs to the consulting rooms and checked in at the busy front desk. The shame of announcing we were here to see a fertility specialist kept me quiet; I let Mark do the talking.

Along the green-carpeted hallway to the waiting room, a waiting room I'd sat in a few times over the years for different reasons. When Bec broke her arm in high school, when I needed my wisdom teeth out, when Dad got his results from a skin cancer he'd had removed from his ear.

This time, another couple sat beneath the window, untouching, the man clutching a bible in both hands. As Mark and I sat, I spotted highlighted passages in the book. His lips moved silently as he read. The woman sat with her eyes downcast, hands clasped in her lap, leaning slightly away from him.

The sight made me ache with an understanding I hadn't

felt before. *This is what it's like*, I thought. *These people have failed at something they wanted, something they thought they were capable of, and it's broken them.*

I reached for Mark, entwining my fingers with his. *In this together.*

The bible-reader and his partner were called in first, and I breathed a sigh of relief once they'd gone.

'You okay?' Mark murmured.

'Did you see them? He was reading the bible.'

He nodded, squeezing my hand a little harder.

'We're not…'

'What?' he whispered.

'I don't know, it's like it's ruined them–'

'No, that's not going to happen to us. That's why we're here now.'

I agreed, loosening my fingers from his. Heat climbed my neck, spreading across my cheeks. I didn't know how to explain to Mark how I felt. What if it was my fault? What if something was wrong with me, and I couldn't ever give him a child?

When the doctor called my name, I stood on trembling legs, fighting panic. Hiding it as best I could, I followed him into his office, Mark trailing behind.

Dr Kemp, a slightly built man with protruding rat-like teeth, sat at an impeccably ordered desk and clicked away at his keyboard. 'Right, I've got a letter from your GP here, and the results from your blood test and pelvic ultrasound…' More tapping at the keyboard. 'All looks okay there. Hormonal levels are normal and no signs of anything in the ultrasound.' He glanced up briefly. 'That's good. So we'll need to get onto some more testing to find out why you're not conceiving.'

I fidgeted in my seat and glanced at Mark.

'So, we've been trying for–' Mark began.

'Yes, yes, I've got the letter here,' the doctor interrupted, glancing up briefly while tapping his computer screen impatiently. 'Now at your ages, I think it's best not to waste any more time. Mark, I'd like to test your sperm, and we all know what's involved there. Emily, in your case it's not as simple. I think it's best to get you straight into the hospital for a laparoscopy.'

'A… what?'

'A laparoscopy. It's a simple procedure, but you will need a general anaesthetic. We'll make two small incisions and have a good look inside to see if there's a reason you're not getting pregnant. The ultrasound was clear but there could be a blockage in your fallopian tubes, for example, and that would explain your infertility.'

'And, um, then what?'

'First things first. But if we don't find a medical reason for your infertility, we can go on to talk about other fertility treatments, like IVF.'

Infertility. Laparoscopy. IVF.

A wave of heat swept up through my body, settling in my head where it beat a hot pulse behind my eyes. I'd had my wisdom teeth out as a teenager, and the experience had been horrible. Apart from that, any reasons for attending the hospital hadn't been related to my own health. And now, this little runt of a man was telling me I needed to get cut open to find out why I couldn't have a baby.

I tried to clear my head to ask more questions. But the doctor beat me to it.

'Right, so I'll get the hospital admissions to call you, Emily. And Mark, this is for you.' He flicked a slip of paper over the smooth desktop. 'We'll catch up again after this is all done and take the next step.'

And with that, he shot backwards in his chair and the appointment was over.

We ordered at the McDonalds drive thru and parked nearby, where the rotunda marked the centre of town. We ate silently, watching people walking by, going about their business. The quiet wasn't awkward, but I felt exhausted after seeing the doctor, drained. And confused that we had to even do this in the first place.

'I'd forgotten how disgusting this food was,' I murmured, wiping a drip of grease from my wrist.

'Not the night to be cooking up a feast, honey. We're both tired.'

'I haven't had Maccas for years. Were the Big Macs always like this?' I indicated the congealed mess of burger in front of me.

Mark smiled with a shake of his head. 'I'm used to it. Some days when I'm busy, it's the quickest thing.'

'Well, it's gross.' I closed the cardboard container on the half-eaten burger. 'So when do you think you'll do your test?' I asked, not looking up, but concentrating on wrestling a soggy French fry into my mouth.

He took a moment to answer. 'We'll talk about that once I've had a chance to think about it.'

I swallowed. 'Okay. So what did you think of Dr Kemp?'

'I thought he was a wanker.'

Laughter burst from me, and I threw my head back against the headrest. 'Thanks for that. I thought so too. It was like we didn't matter at all. But he is supposed to be the best.'

Mark grinned along with me, demolishing the remainder of my burger. I sat silently beside him, waiting for him to finish his meal. I watched people pass by the car, groups of loud kids and young parents with prams. And an elderly couple, strolling hand in hand with contented smiles.

I kissed Mark's greasy lips. *No matter what, we'll be okay.*

Chapter 6

Friday night rolled around again, and this time we decided to meet at *The Flying Dragon* restaurant. I'd roped in Mark and Travis to join us, as well as Patrick. Mark had complained for the last few days about having to sit down to a meal with my boss.

I made less effort when dressing this time, leaving my hair out and choosing a clean pair of jeans, plain top and leather jacket. Bec and Travis picked us up, and we arrived ten minutes late, expecting that Patrick and Victoria would already be inside.

We opened the restaurant door and entered under the red-painted dragon tail. Ahead a long, dark tiled hallway led to the bistro, our footsteps echoing as we pounded along. Soft music reached our ears, and a mass of hastily decorated tables blocked our path. I scanned the restaurant and found Victoria and Patrick sitting side by side at a large table by the buffet. There was nothing in their body language right then to suggest they were romantically involved; they weren't touching, and Victoria was looking around and not at him.

Her gaze settled on Mark, and the look she gave him had my world fall away, the music dimmed, and I felt my throat tighten. Then she looked at me, and smiled.

I turned to Bec, but she and Travis were already weaving their way towards the table, and she hadn't noticed. Mark and I followed, and we took the last two seats at the table. We greeted each other over the Lazy Susan, and under the table, I jabbed Bec in the thigh. She jabbed me back.

'Nice to see you, Bec. You look good.' Patrick grinned at my sister.

'Whatever,' she mumbled, picking up the menu. Opening it, she peered over the top of it at Victoria. 'So, how are you settling in?'

Victoria directed a dazzling smile across the table. 'Really well. Emily has made me feel so welcome, as has Pat, of course.'

Bec quirked an eyebrow. '*Pat* likes to make the ladies welcome.' Travis and Mark burst out laughing, and a second later, the rest of us followed, including Patrick. 'You're from Sydney, right?'

Victoria nodded, and daintily picked up her own menu.

'Em said you've got a young daughter back there?'

Victoria fumbled the menu and slapped it back on the tabletop. 'Yes, I do. She's with my mum but coming down to live with me.'

Bec shot a glance at me. 'That's nice. We've got a little girl as well. Poppy.'

Victoria nodded vigorously, her eyes brightening. 'I'd love to meet her sometime.'

Again, Bec's eyes flicked to mine. 'That would be nice.'

A waitress appeared at the table and we ordered food

and drinks. I picked random items from the menu, half-listening to the conversations around the table. Patrick was trying to engage the boys by talking about sport, and Mark – bless him – was hanging in there. Travis didn't like Patrick either, but he didn't seem to think about it too much, so he was doing a lot of the talking. Bec was asking more questions about Victoria's life in Sydney, which she seemed to be deflecting by asking Bec questions instead.

I tried to focus on my food, but couldn't help notice Victoria's flirting. Whenever there was a lull in conversation, I watched her zero-in on my husband, asking him questions about his work, about his family, where he went to school. At one point she picked up a greasy spring roll and wrapped her lips around it, all the while keeping her eyes on Mark. I stabbed at my lemon chicken, not believing what I was seeing.

Or was I imagining her attempts at seduction? Was I that insecure about this woman that I didn't want my husband to be around her?

Taking a bathroom break, I sat on the loo and took some deep breaths. I couldn't help but feel disgusted at myself. Even if Victoria did find Mark attractive, what the hell did that even mean? It wasn't as if he'd ever do anything. This was about my job, and nothing else. She was a colleague; a beautiful one, yes, and she was possibly sleeping with the boss, but I needed to be comfortable and confident in myself, in my marriage. Nothing else mattered. Taking another breath, I let myself out of the cubicle and washed my hands. I waited a few minutes, smoothing my hair with my fingers, hoping that Bec would follow me in and then I could ask her what she thought about Victoria's behaviour. But the thought that it could be Victoria instead who followed me in had me moving out of the bathroom and back into the hot, loud bistro.

At home, the four of us sat in the lounge dissecting the evening.

'Yes, she flirts. Not just with Mark but with my man too.' Bec slung a protective arm over Travis's shoulder.

'Aw, you're jealous? I can't help it if I appeal to the ladies. Just born that way, I guess.'

Bec rolled her eyes at her husband. 'And she is very pretty.'

'Pretty?' I repeated. 'She's beautiful, don't you think? Almost unnaturally so. She belongs on TV or something.'

'Why does she bother you so much?' Mark asked. He asked the question almost lazily, but I could sense the annoyance in the words. He was sick of hearing about her, but he didn't understand. He didn't know Patrick the way I did, and didn't understand the way women could compete with each other. I didn't like it either; it wasn't as though I wanted to talk about her, but that choice was taken out of my hands when Patrick hired her.

'And what do you think about her and Patrick?' I asked Bec and Travis, ignoring Mark's question.

'You mean *Pat?*' Bec smirked.

'I know!' I cried. 'What the hell?'

'You think they're sleeping together?' Bec asked me.

I nodded. 'Don't you?'

Bec bit her lip. 'Yeah, I think they probably are.'

Told you so, I wanted to say to Mark, but I kept quiet.

'She was more nervous than I expected,' Bec added,

frowning. 'Questions seem to make her uncomfortable, like when I asked about her daughter.'

I took a sip of water, thinking over what Bec said. 'That's true. She's weird when talking about her own life.'

Mark chuckled. 'You're really searching for a reason not to like her, aren't you?'

I glared at him, and he shrunk back a little.

'Hey, Em,' Travis interrupted. 'How come you're not drinking lately? You don't have any news to share, do you?'

'Travis!' Bec cried. 'What the hell is wrong with you? You really think it's okay to say that? Like not drinking automatically means that? Jesus Christ, she doesn't have to drink every single night like you do!'

Travis sighed loudly and stood. 'Marky Mark, our work is done. Both wives are officially pissed off. Time to head on home.'

I dreamt about cats. A bunch of different coloured cats lined up along the fence outside our bedroom window. The moon cast them in an eerie light, and their eyes beamed out fluorescent green through the dark. I watched from behind the glass as they stood completely still staring back at me, their eyes piercing into me. They didn't move, and I couldn't look away. One by one their mouths opened, spilling out the wail of an air-raid siren.

Kicking at the bed sheet, I sat up in the dark, breathing hard. Beside me, Mark snored softly, one arm flung up over his head. Quietly, I crept out of bed and pulled back the curtain. The fence was farther away than in my dream but despite this I could tell in the moonlight that nothing sat atop it. Obviously, there weren't any cats with glowing eyes screeching at me.

I ran my hands through my hair. It was knotted and damp with sweat. The clock read 4:26. Too early to get up, too late to get suitable rest. *Shit.* I got up anyway, chucking on a pair of shorts and t-shirt and creeping out into the lounge room, where I slid the door shut behind me.

The house was hot and still. Opening a window, I held my hand against the screen but couldn't feel any breeze. Another stinker on its way then. Navigating my way through hulking shadows, I found a nearby lamp switch, and a soft yellow light bloomed. In the kitchen, I filled my coffee pot with water, spooned coffee into the filter and sat it on the stove top. I rubbed my eyes and yawned as it heated and bubbled.

It was *way* too early for a Saturday morning. How I longed to crawl back into bed and curl into Mark, but I was too hot and agitated. With my mug in hand, I fired up my laptop and sat at the kitchen table, sipping. I logged into Facebook, typed "Victoria Shafer" into the search bar. There were several, but none of the pictures were her. I swore at myself, and pushed my computer away. Carrying my mug with me, I tiptoed outside and sat on the back step.

Surveying the backyard in the dark, I sipped my coffee and sighed. So Victoria liked men and didn't like to talk about her daughter, so what? Maybe she had a shaky relationship with her mother, and didn't like leaving her daughter behind with her? Maybe her uneasiness had something to do with the girl's father? It was really none of my business.

I leaned back against the door with a sigh and drained my mug.

It was eerily still. The warm night air stuck to my bare

legs like syrup. I wriggled my toes, feeling grains of dirt from the step but no breeze at all. The shrubs against the fence were shadows in the dark, nothing more. The clothesline was invisible. To my right, the back shed was a just looming shape, edges indistinct. The air held the threat of a storm, a heaviness that put me on alert. I scanned the yard once more, but nothing moved, not at all. I climbed the step and slipped back inside.

I glanced at my computer as I rinsed my mug in the sink, but I wasn't in the right frame of mind to go online. Once I started start digging into Victoria's personal life… well, I didn't want to be that person. I had a little job at a gallery and a man who loved me at home. One of those things was way more important than the other. With that, I rifled through the pantry, pulling out a bag of flour and some caster sugar. From the fridge, I retrieved a carton of eggs, stick of butter and bottle of milk. Okay, it was way too hot to bake, but it was best to do it before the heat of the day struck.

Grabbing a wooden spoon, I smiled to myself as I thought of my nanna. She taught me to bake when I was younger, and I had loved nothing more than sitting in her kitchen watching her measure the ingredients. When Mark and I met, she knew he was the one, and also that she didn't have much time left. She'd told me, 'If he comes home and you've been baking or you've made him a nice meal, he'll forgive you for anything.' Her advice made me wonder what she'd done to Grandpa that needed forgiving, but I didn't ask.

Once I'd lined the tin, I spooned in the cake mixture and washed some fresh berries, slicing the strawberries and arranging them on top with the raspberries and blueberries.

With a final sprinkle of sugar on top, I slid the cake into the oven.

The smell of baking soon filled the house. I found a hair elastic among the detritus on the coffee table and tied up my hair. I was sweaty and sticky, but didn't want to switch on the air conditioner so early in the morning. I opened the windows one by one, hovering by the large floor-to-ceiling one in the lounge room, praying for a breeze. Nothing. I blew out a breath, surveying the slowly lightening street through the glass. Mrs Nichol's house across the way was still shut down for the night; she was an early riser, out in the garden every time I happened to be up at dawn. But not this morning. A car was at her kerb though, one I hadn't seen before. Her sons visited from time to time, and they both had 4WD vehicles covered in dust, family stickers on the back windscreen, numerous kids spilling from the doors. This was a sedan of some sort, slightly fancy, shiny and clean-looking, even though it was still too dark to pick out the colour.

Shit. Mrs Nichol is the stickybeak, not me. I clucked my tongue and stepped away from the window, sinking into the couch and resting my head back. I wasn't liking this new version of myself. I'd never been catty. Bec either. We'd stuck together at school, avoiding the bitchy girls and preferring to hang out with the boys, or at least the girls who were interesting or sporty, rather than arrogant and shallow. Bec and I were so alike in this way that even Mrs Nichol, who had known us since we were kids, often mixed up our names. 'Good morning, Rebecca dear,' she'd say, and after a while I'd simply stopped correcting her. It was much easier just to smile and wave.

By the time the cake was out of the oven, I had given up on a natural breeze and shut the windows. I flicked on the air conditioner and basked in the cool air by standing right in front of the unit. That's where Mark found me, lifting up my t-shirt and swivelling from side to side to air my armpits.

'Aren't you a sight for sore eyes?'

'At least you know how lucky you are.'

We kissed, and he lifted his nose and sniffed.

'The cake I hope, not my BO?'

He laughed. 'No, it's definitely a good smell. You made a cake?' His eyes flicked to the clock. 'At six am?'

I nodded. 'Couldn't sleep.'

'Everything okay?'

'Yep.' I took his hand and led him to the kitchen, where the cake was cooling on a rack by the sink.

'Good, then cut me a chuck of that, yeah?'

I obliged, and switched on the hotplate to heat the coffee I'd prepared for him earlier.

'I love it when you bake, perfect wife that you are.'

I flicked him with a tea towel, passing him a plate with a large slab of cake on it. He closed his eyes while he ate, and I watched him, thinking again of Nanna's advice.

'Any plans for today?' he asked, licking his finger and collecting crumbs.

'Nope. Thought we could go to the beach? If you want.'

'Come to bed first.' He wiggled his eyebrows, and I laughed at him.

'No, I'm all sweaty and gross.'

'I don't care.' He tugged at me, and I had just enough time to turn off the stove before he picked me up and carried me to the bedroom.

Hot, exhausted, and covered in sand, we left the queue at the kiosk with our ice cream and headed for the car. The beach had been packed with families and picnic rugs and a small-scale cricket match. We'd toasted ourselves on our towels for a while, reading and sipping from our water bottles. But the sun had beat down relentlessly, and we'd chased each other into the surf, drifting on frothy-topped waves amongst the bobbing heads of other swimmers.

I sucked my dripping ice cream as Mark drove the familiar road. The road I took when I needed to escape. It was a comforting drive and, after all, Mark and I had met on this beach. It meant a lot to us; a place where I could escape reality and switch off.

Mark pulled into the driveway, and we waved to Mrs Nichol who was out in her garden in her giant sun hat. The car from this morning was gone, so maybe she'd had an overnight guest. Mark eased the car into the garage; it was stinking hot inside, and we cursed as we fumbled our way into the house with our towels and beach bag.

The house felt a bit cooler, the ceramic tiles a relief against our bare feet. Mark trotted off to the shower while I unpacked the bag and chucked our wet towels into the washing machine. Pausing in the laundry doorway, I peered through into the kitchen, a shiver creeping up my spine. Something didn't seem right.

I scanned the room, taking in the potted peace lily on the bench, the pile of bills and appointment letters beside it, the dish rack full of dishes, the coffee pot still on the stove from this morning. Everything was in its place, so why did I feel anxious? I walked around the room, feeling silly. A magnet of Poppy's face was the only thing on the fridge; I opened it. The cake was covered in Glad wrap, the peaches and plums and nectarines filled the drawers at the bottom. The door was lined with bottles of beer. Everything normal.

I shook my head.

Left the room.

Made my way to the bathroom so I could wash off the grains of sand.

Chapter 7

Monday morning, a cup of steaming coffee was already waiting on my desk. Victoria flicked through canvases stacked against the wall of Patrick's office, oohing and aahing dramatically. When she saw me, however, she trotted out, indicating the coffee with a big smile on her face.

'Thanks.' I lifted the cup and took a sip. 'Appreciate it.'

'Well, I wanted to tell you how nice it was on Friday night. You guys are all so friendly.'

I swallowed. The coffee was perfect.

'I'm looking forward to doing that again, and Bec bringing that gorgeous little girl of hers,' she gushed.

'When's your daughter coming? The girls could play together.'

Victoria's eyes glazed a little, and a dreamy smile spread across her face. 'Yes. I'd like that. My baby needs a friend.'

My mobile vibrated in my bag, snapping my attention away. I reached for it, noted the 'Private Number' display and quickly left the office.

'Hello?'

'Hello, is that Emily?'

'Yes.' I pushed through the back door of the gallery, closing it quietly behind me. Outside, I sank on to the concrete steps. The sun belted down, heating my head and shoulders.

'This is Janet calling from Admissions at the hospital. I have a referral here from Dr Kemp for a laparoscopy, and we can get you in this Friday morning if that suits you?'

My chin quivered, so I bit down on my lip a moment. '*This* Friday?'

'That's right. Dr Kemp comes up once a month and he's had a cancellation. Can you come up Friday morning?'

'I... I guess I can, yes,' I stammered. 'What do I need to do?'

I hugged my knees as Janet went over the details, and I tried to commit them to memory. After hanging up, I sat for a moment, staring out over the small car park behind the gallery, the black tar surface of the dead-end road shimmering in the heat.

That afternoon before I left work, I slipped into Patrick's office and closed the door behind me. He looked up from his computer screen, eyebrows raised. 'Private meeting?'

I sighed, lingering opposite his desk impatiently. 'It's late notice, but I need to have Friday off if that's okay.'

He sniffed and leaned back in his creaking leather chair. 'Sure. Everything all right?'

'Thanks. Everything's okay, I just have a doctor's appointment that was sprung on me, and I can't really change it.'

'No worries. Victoria's here, so no drama. See, I told you another assistant would come in handy.' He grinned, running his fingers over the edge of the shiny desk. His fingernails were long, shapely and buffed to a high sheen.

My mouth twisted. 'Thanks, Patrick. Appreciate it.'

I backed out of the office and almost ran into Victoria, who was crouched near the kitchen, taping up boxes. 'Whoops!' she chirped. I forced a smile and retrieved my bag, trying to ignore my thumping heartbeat. I rarely took a day off, and didn't want Patrick to realise he could manage just fine without me.

#

'Friday? This Friday?'

We sat in the backyard in the dusky light. The dry grass tickled my bare feet, crickets chirped. Over the fence, the smell of sizzling sausages drifted, children giggled. I didn't know their names; they'd only moved in a couple of months ago.

'He's had a cancellation apparently.'

'Wow, okay.'

'Can you get the day off? Because I'm sure Bec would–'

'No, no, I'll get the day off. Of course I will.'

'Okay.'

I lay back on the grass and stretched. Mark propped my feet in his lap and rubbed the soles with his thumbs in slow circles.

'Don't get me used to this,' I murmured. 'Or I'll be asking for it every night.'

Mark chuckled. 'You can ask me for whatever you want.'

'How about this? I think it's time we put a deck out here,'

I said, swatting at a mosquito.

'Yeah, you've mentioned that before.'

'So let's do it.'

'Okay, moneybags,' he laughed.

I laughed too, staring up as the stars blinked on, one by one. 'Fair point.'

'Plus we're renting, remember. We just can't go doing that stuff.'

I killed another mosquito and flicked its corpse into the grass. 'Oh, they won't care as long as we pay for it.'

We fell silent and I gazed up at the sky, day dimming into night. Mark's massage was helping release the stress of the day, and I closed my eyes, finally relaxing.

After a while, Mark's voice broke the spell. 'I did my test today.'

I sat up, tucking my feet under me. 'What?'

Mark shrugged, although it was hard to see him now in the dwindling light. 'In my lunch break.'

'Why didn't you tell me you were doing it today? I could have met you somewhere, or–'

'That's why,' Mark interrupted. 'I didn't want you to make it a big deal. And I didn't know I was doing it today anyway. I just decided to do it in the spur of the moment.'

'You don't think it's a big deal?'

Mark sighed. 'That's not what I meant. But I can't worry about this every day of my life, Em. It's just getting too big now. I have to think about other things, do other things.'

My cheeks warmed; my belly flipped. I couldn't help feeling hurt. 'You think I'm obsessing?'

'No,' Mark reached for my hand and pulled me closer to him. 'You're not, but don't you think it could easily become like that? I don't want this to overtake all the good stuff we've got.'

'Well, neither do I. And I'm not doing that. I've made a point of not going online to look up stuff. And you had to push me to make an appointment with that doctor, I didn't even want to.'

'I know,' Mark soothed. 'You're doing great, honey. But I had to do this by myself, and not make a big deal about it, okay? And when it comes to you, I'll be there with you because it's a much bigger deal.'

I rubbed my belly. 'I don't want it to be a big deal.'

Mark didn't answer, just squeezed my hand a little tighter.

'We haven't even talked about what we'll do if they find something wrong,' I said, my voice cracking. 'I don't think I could do IVF or anything like that.'

Mark bit his lip. 'Hopefully, we won't have to talk about that.'

'Are we being stupid though, Mark? We don't know much at all about what could be wrong.'

'No,' he answered, a little loudly. 'We're trying to keep things simple, aren't we? And even now with these tests, we just need to relax and take things one step at a time. Try to keep things normal. That was our plan.'

I nodded, yet there was niggling doubt. I was trying so hard not to obsess, to make love thinking of Mark, and not the possibility of making a baby. And despite the fact I hadn't researched, details still reached me in my daily life: diets women had undertaken, IVF struggles, hormone injections, charting body temperatures. This information floated on the breeze. I overheard things on the street, in interviews and ads on television… I tried not to listen; I didn't want to go down that path. And it was clear Mark didn't want to either.

But I had bought things for the baby and packed them away. Mark was making a cot in the garage. We'd kept the spare room empty on purpose, and I wondered if we should have done that. We'd already made room for a baby who didn't even exist yet, and might not ever. And sweet Poppy… we had a gorgeous niece who was a painful reminder of what we wanted and didn't have. How could we just *ignore* all of that and not obsess? We were seeing a doctor now, and I'd be having surgery soon. Our wait-and-see phase had ended, whether Mark wanted to believe it or not.

#

Mark and I walked into the Day Procedure unit. My heart was pounding; I didn't know what to expect.

After checking in, a nurse led us to a curtained cubicle and instructed me to change into a gown. 'Undies off,' she said, nodding and whisking the curtain closed as she left. Her shoes squeaked away over the linoleum.

'I didn't recognise her,' I said to Mark as I stripped off. 'We're going to run into someone we know, aren't we? Imagine if Mum finds out and I haven't told her what's happening today.'

'Is that really what you're worried about right now?' He rubbed my shoulders. 'Honey, we deal with that if it happens okay?'

'But it's a small town. Word gets around about these things.'

He rubbed a hand over his face. 'We knew it would be

hard to keep this a secret. If it happens, it happens.' He tied the strings at the back of my gown.

I crawled on to the bed and crossed my legs, tugging at the material to cover myself.

Mark came to sit beside me. 'Are you okay? Not too nervous?'

I stared into his eyes that looked a little wide, with dark shadows beneath them. His face was pale. '*You* look nervous.'

He puffed out his cheeks. 'I am. I just wish that if there was going to be something… wrong… that it would be with me.'

'Why? You tested fine, you should be happy.'

'No,' he said, shaking his head. 'The last thing I want is to see you upset.'

My heart swelled and as I reached over to hold him, a face poked through the curtain. An uncertain smile. 'Oh, hi… Emily.' The curtain was drawn back. 'I'm Eddie. I'll be taking you into theatre.' He stood awkwardly in his blue scrubs, clipboard in hand. 'Are you ready?'

I nodded, and Mark squeezed my fingers for a moment before he moved away.

'Make yourself comfortable,' Eddie said. 'We need to check your details first.'

I arranged myself under the stiff, cold sheet and let Eddie do his thing, taping on my ID bracelet and answering his questions. When it was time to go, I couldn't suppress a frightened swivel in Mark's direction as Eddie wheeled me away. Mark stood by the curtain, hands in pockets, looking somewhat lost.

In the theatre, Dr Kemp treated me to a cursory pat on the knee and then I was being moved onto the operating table. My legs were spread, feet propped on a flat surface I couldn't see, and another man I didn't recognise appeared at my left, readying the anaesthetic. My heart was beating a little too fast so I focused on slowing it down as a couple of other nurses entered in fresh-looking scrubs. Eddie's face loomed over me. 'You feeling okay?'

I nodded, not trusting my voice to answer.

'We're going to give you something to help you relax now,' said the man to my left, and I looked at him for a moment, nodding. He reached for my hand and I knew he was injecting something, something that didn't seem to be making much difference to anything…

Bang.

My eyes snapped open.

I tried to sit up, but a nurse appeared, her kindly face hovering above mine. 'Welcome back, Emily. It's all over now.'

Turning my head on the pillow, I noticed I was in a different room with several other patients on their own trolleys. I couldn't see Mark and I wanted to ask the nurse, but my mouth wasn't working.

'My name is Diane,' she continued, her voice soft and reassuring. 'You're in recovery now, and very soon we'll take you back to your husband.'

Okay. Thank you, I wanted to say, but stayed quiet. My eyelids began to drift closed again but I fought the instinct, stretching my eyes wide open.

'You probably still feel a bit sleepy, but that's just the anaesthetic wearing off. It's totally normal.' Diane patted my hand. Her lined face was familiar, auburn curls just visible at the edges of her cap. 'I know your mum, you know.'

Oh no.

'We used to play tennis together at the club. A few years ago now. But my husband was retiring and suddenly I didn't have time for tennis anymore.' She laughed, a tinkling sound that hurt my ears. 'He's bought a caravan, and we're taking trips up the coast when I can get time off.'

I tried my voice. 'My mum doesn't…' I croaked, but couldn't finish.

She seemed to understand, flapping a hand. 'Oh, I've worked here a long time. I don't gossip, love.'

Smiling in response, I relaxed, letting my eyes close. Just for a moment.

Chapter 8

Next time I opened my eyes, Mark was sitting by the bed, and we were back in the cubicle with the curtain surrounding us.

He lurched up, grinning. 'You're awake!'

I smiled back. 'So thirsty,' I croaked. He helped me sip from a cup of water on the bedside table.

'You feel all right?'

I nodded, swallowing all the water. 'I'm not in any pain.'

'Good. Dr Kemp came by just before, but you were still asleep so he said he'd come back. He said everything went well.'

'What does that mean?'

Mark shrugged, but his face looked untroubled. 'Don't know but sounds promising.' He eased beside me on the narrow mattress, filled my cup with more water from a plastic jug on the bedside table. Through the curtain to my left, I could hear a woman quietly sobbing, and a male voice attempting to soothe her. I looked at Mark, and could tell he was listening too.

Within seconds, my curtain was eased open and Dr Kemp stepped through. Was he the man giving another patient bad news? My heart skipped a beat. The poor woman. Was that going to be me in a few minutes?

'Emily, how are you feeling?'

I nodded at him. 'Okay, thanks.'

'Good. The procedure went well. I checked everything thoroughly, including your fallopian tubes and your ovaries. There aren't any blockages, cysts or tumours, basically no reason I could find to explain why you can't get pregnant.' Mark and I glanced at each other, and I allowed myself a small smile. 'What this means,' Dr Kemp continued, 'is that your infertility is unexplained. There's no medical reason. So we need to get started on some fertility treatment to help you along.'

My smile faded. 'What kind of treatment? Do you mean IVF?'

He shook his head. 'I wouldn't start there. A drug such as Clomid is usually the best place to start. You can look it up online in the meantime, but if we meet in about a month's time, I'll go over everything with you both then.' He paused, raising his eyebrows. 'Okay? Any other questions?'

I floundered. It was Mark who spoke. 'Four weeks sounds good. Thanks, Doc.'

'Just take it easy for a few days. You should stop bleeding after a week or so.' Dr Kemp disappeared through the curtain, and Mark and I were once again enveloped by fabric privacy.

'Fertility treatment. Fucking hell,' I whispered. 'I thought at first it was good news, but it's not really, is it?'

'It *is* good news, honey,' Mark reassured me, helping me

to sit up in bed. 'He didn't find anything scary. That's great news.'

I let out a big breath. 'That's true. Okay. I shouldn't think about this now, the drugs. Right?' Gingerly, I reached between my legs and felt some thick padding. My fingers came away stained with blood.

Mark flinched. 'Shit, are you sore?'

'No, I just feel gross. Do you think I can get dressed, or do I have to lay here?'

Mark helped me waddle across the hospital car park, and climb into the car. Dressing hadn't been too pleasant, but I'd used tissues to tidy up as best I could while Mark helped me into my pants. I longed to shower, to wash away the antiseptic and surgical blood, to snuggle up in warm pjs on the couch. Despite the summer heat, the sterile environment in the hospital had left me feeling chilled.

At home, Mark microwaved frozen dinners while I cleaned up. I swaddled myself in a cotton blanket on the couch, relishing the closed-up warmth of the house. We ate side by side, Mark quiet and frequently glancing across at me. Eventually, I put down my fork and glared at him. 'Stop looking at me. I'm fine.'

'Sorry. Just checking.' His lips cracked into a smile. 'Geez.'

I laughed. 'Really, I'm okay. I don't feel much pain or anything. It's like period cramps, that's all.'

He nodded, seemingly comforted by this information. 'Good. Okay.' He continued eating, before glancing at me one more time.

I sighed. 'What?'

This time he didn't smile. 'I'm just thinking about that woman next door, you know, how he must have given her some bad news.'

My eyes filled. I blinked the tears away. 'Me too. And I should be pleased, *we* should be pleased that there's nothing wrong with us. But I'm just thinking how we still need fertility treatment. This isn't over, there's still no reason why it's not happening.' I shook my head, imagining the emotion flicking away like the water droplets from the still-wet strands of my hair.

'Can I get you anything else to eat? We can have toast, or cereal, or–'

'No, I'm okay.'

'Movie? TV? I could get your Kindle?'

I smiled. 'Since you're offering. My Kindle, and a cup of tea?'

He picked up our empty plates. 'You're still cold?'

I hunkered down under the blanket, tucking a cushion under my head. 'Yeah, the hospital was freezing.'

Mark clattered through into the kitchen, and I listened as he filled the kettle, humming as he pulled out a mug, opened the fridge. Pressing a hand against my cramping belly, I curled on my side.

#

Bec arrived early the next morning, hammering on our bedroom window and startling me out of a fitful sleep. Mark, already up, let her in. I stared at the bedroom ceiling, where the sun painted yellow lines across it, until the bedroom door squeaked open and Bec crawled on to the bed holding a mug of coffee and bowl of fruit salad.

'I've brought treats.'

Arranging the pillows behind me, I sat up and accepted my breakfast.

Bec settled next to me, propping her chin in hand. 'How are you feeling?'

'I feel okay. A few cramps.'

'Bleeding?'

I nodded, popping a chunk of pineapple in my mouth. 'For a week or so they said.'

'I'm so glad there's nothing wrong, Em.'

'Me too.' Glancing across at her, I noticed her eyes had filled with tears. 'Change the subject. Tell me something.'

Bec sniffed, reaching for a tissue from the box beside the bed. 'Okay, here's something. I saw Victoria last night. I took Poppy to pick up a pizza and she came into the shop behind us. You should have seen her with Poppy, she was all over her like a rash.' Bec laughed and blew her nose. 'Anyway, she knew you had a medical thing going on.'

'She did?' I sipped my coffee. 'Oh, Patrick must have said something. I think I told him I was seeing a doctor.'

'Oh, well… I don't remember exactly, but I'm sure she mentioned something about you having a procedure.'

I certainly didn't tell Patrick that. I wouldn't have told him that. So how would Victoria know? Taking another sip, I frowned over the rim of the mug. 'I don't like them gossiping about me. It feels like it's just a matter of time before I'm out on my arse.'

'Don't be silly.' Bec plucked a chunk of watermelon out of the bowl and popped it into her mouth. 'Worst case scenario, you get another job. You've gotta focus on what's most important to you, and that's being a mum.' She raised an eyebrow. 'Right?'

'Yes,' I smiled. 'Thanks for cutting through the crap.'

'You're very welcome. Are you coming for lunch tomorrow or will you make an excuse?'

'No, I'm coming. It's just easier.'

Bec nodded. 'Good.'

#

After lunch at Mum and Dad's, I went home with Bec to look after Poppy so Bec and Travis could go to their CFA meeting to discuss hazard reduction and the upcoming weather forecast. I was so proud they were volunteer firefighters, but I still worried about them.

I said goodbye to Mark and climbed into the car next to my niece. Travis sang along to the Wiggles as he spun the wheel effortlessly down the gravel road towards the farmhouse.

'Hot potato, hot potato!' Poppy squawked, hyper after sucking on several red icy poles. I laughed at her, dodging the stale cracker fragments as I danced with her in the back seat. Travis sprayed dust, stopping the car right by the front door.

'Put a motor on it, Bec, don't wanna be late.'

'You don't have to tell me that,' she snapped, unbuckling Poppy's car seat.

'Just go,' I interrupted, waving her hand away. 'Go get ready, I'll take care of this.'

'Thanks,' she called, already up the steps and thumping along the wooden veranda. The black painted front door stood open, catching the sunlight as Bec barrelled through it. I unhooked Poppy from the seat, lifting her down to the gravel driveway. 'Well, we're home, sweetheart. What do you want to do while Mum and Dad are at their meeting?'

'I wanna play princesses!' she cried, twirling towards the steps.

'Of course you do!' I dashed after her, grabbing her under the arms to swing her up the steps.

Inside the house, the curtains were shut, casting the kitchen and lounge room into shadow. I threw the heavy drapes open, wincing against the dust that flew through the air. The room was a mess, strewn with Poppy's stuff: colouring books, dolls and teddies, crayons, clothes, and the occasional crusty coffee mug. *This is what it's all about, the chaos of life with a child. This is what will happen to us once we have a kid.* I grabbed a handful of dirty cups and deposited them in the kitchen beside piles of other dirty dishes.

'Sorry about the mess,' Bec muttered, running past and picking up her handbag. 'Just leave it.' She bent down to scoop up her daughter, who had flopped on the carpet to play with her dolls. 'You be good for Aunty Emily, okay? Daddy and I will be home later.' Bec turned to me. 'We're taking the ute, so use the car if you need it.'

'Sure thing.'

'And there's some leftover tuna casserole and salad in the fridge for dinner.'

'Yuck!' Poppy stuck out her tongue and I tried not to laugh.

'No time to argue,' Bec replied, plopping her daughter

back on the carpet. She pecked me on the cheek and rushed to the front door where Travis called out his goodbyes. Once the door slammed shut, I lowered myself to my knees. 'Okay, pumpkin. You want to have a rest before we play?'

Poppy stuck out her bottom lip, as though thinking hard. 'Movie?'

I nodded. 'Go pick one.'

We settled on the couch with a *My Little Pony* DVD. Ten minutes in and I was incredibly bored, but Poppy's rapt attention had me smiling. Eyeing the room, I was eager to get up and clean, but I stayed put. Poppy's little hands were folded in her lap, her legs crossed at the ankles. I took in her features, so like Bec and mine when we were little. Snub nose, wide eyes with long lashes. She pouted when concentrating, highlighting a dimple in her chin. Her blonde curls were frizzed from another busy day running around, a ladybug hair clip coming loose. I fixed it and she glanced up briefly before returning her attention to the pastel-coloured shapes on the screen. If I let myself, I could imagine that she was my own daughter. But I stayed focused on the hurt in my heart, reminding myself that she wasn't, that despite the good result from the operation, there may never be a child.

After we'd played princesses for a long hour, I convinced Poppy it was time to rest with our dinner. We sat out on the back veranda with our bowls of tuna casserole on the picnic table.

'I don't like it,' Poppy grunted.

'There's ice cream for dessert if you eat your dinner.'

She grunted again and pushed away her pink plastic fork.

'Pops, you'll make Mum very happy if you eat your dinner. We don't want Mummy to be grumpy, do we?'

Poppy looked up with pursed lips, thinking, then shook her head. 'I eat some.'

'Good girl.'

She lifted her fork and picked at the noodles. I sat back, eating from my own bowl. Across the paddock, I watched the long grass sway in the breeze, the sun lightening the blades into a straw yellow. Travis didn't tend to the paddocks too much, but the yard around the house was immaculate. The edges trimmed all over, a well-structured vegie garden full of lettuce and tomatoes, fruit trees by the wire fence overflowing with plums. Poppy had a swing set, slide and sandpit, a pink plastic tent set up where she liked to play picnics. A rustic stone path led to a clothesline turning gently, white sheets swaying in the air.

'Done.'

I frowned at Poppy. She'd only eaten half from the small bowl. I held up one finger and she obeyed, shovelling a final forkful into her mouth with a grimace.

I put Poppy to bed fresh from her bath, her hair towel-dried and smelling of baby shampoo.

'Goodnight, sweet girl. You call out if you need me, okay?'

She nodded sleepily, burrowing under the sheet. 'Love you.'

Tears pricked my eyes. 'Love you too, honey.'

The sun was lowering but the evening was still hot. I collected the sheets from the line, inhaling the scent of sunshine as I carried them inside and folded them. I loaded the dishwasher, not bothering to rinse anything, and switched on the machine. In the lounge room, I picked up Poppy's toys and dumped them into a plastic toy box. Spying the crumbs on the carpet, I longed to vacuum, but I didn't want to wake Poppy and my stomach was cramping. Dr Kemp had told me to rest for a few days after the operation, and I hadn't obeyed. Sinking gently into the couch, I pressed a hand against my belly and closed my eyes.

'Emileee!'

I shot up off the couch and ran. In Poppy's room, she sat clutching the sheet to her chin, eyes so wide they filled half her face.

'What is it?'

'There's a lady in my room.'

Chapter 9

Flicking on the lamp beside her bed, I sat beside her on the mattress. 'It's okay, Pops. There's just me here, see?'

She shook her head, eyes brimming with tears. 'No!' She pointed to the window. 'She went out there!'

The breeze stirred the curtain and I stood warily, stepping towards the window. Peering through the fly wire, I scanned the backyard. It was almost dark now; my eyes picked out shadows and analysed them. Despite not seeing anything suspicious, I couldn't help feeling unnerved. This wasn't my house, and I was responsible for a little girl not my own.

'There's no one there, Pops,' I whispered.

She stared up at me, all innocence with her wide eyes.

I slammed the window shut and flicked the lock. 'How about I stay here with you until Mum and Dad get home?'

She nodded quickly.

I wiped her eyes. 'Just give me a sec.'

Walking quickly through the house, I locked all the doors and checked the windows. In the front yard, I froze as something moved along the fence. Narrowing my eyes, I looked hard through the glass, but I couldn't see it anymore. Probably an animal.

In Poppy's room, I crawled onto her bed and lay down beside her. She nestled against my chest, quaking. I held her close.

#

Someone touched my shoulder.

I jolted awake.

Bec grinned down at me. 'Morning.'

Rubbing my eyes, I sat up. Beside me, Poppy was sprawled face down, sheet kicked free. 'Hi. Pops had a bad dream, I think.'

Bec frowned. 'Really? She's usually such a good sleeper.'

I followed my sister quietly out of Poppy's room and into the kitchen. 'How was the meeting?'

Bec's mouth twisted. 'We're expecting a hot couple of weeks ahead. Fire bans galore. It's too risky to do hazard reduction burns now, so we'll have to be right onto things.'

'Shit, like it's not hot enough already?'

Bec laughed. 'Exactly.'

Travis passed through the kitchen, smiling hello as he went. 'Poppy give you any trouble?'

'No, of course not.'

'She had a bad dream though, Em said.'

'Really?' he stopped. 'What about?'

I leaned against the bench. 'She said there was a lady in her room. Freaked me out a bit actually. She got pretty upset.'

Travis and Bec glanced at each other.

'What?'

'She said the same thing last night,' Bec said. 'That's weird. Why would she get that into her head?'

I crossed my arms, suppressing a shiver. 'I checked all the doors and everything, and I thought I saw something move out in the front yard, but–'

'Jesus!' Bec cried, slapping a hand to her chest.

'No, no,' I flapped my hand at her, trying to calm her down. 'I'm sure it was just an animal. It was dusk, it was nothing, I'm positive. But she wanted me to stay with her until she fell asleep.'

'Probably a roo,' Travis murmured.

The dishwasher beeped, and the noise broke the tension. Bec stared around the kitchen. 'You cleaned! I told you to leave it.'

'You're welcome,' I smiled.

'Want a drink?' Travis pulled a beer out of the fridge and held it out to me.

'No, I might get a lift home if that's okay. I don't feel the best.' I fought the urge to hold my aching abdomen.

'You do look pale.' Bec pressed a palm to my forehead, and held my gaze. Her eyes asked the question we didn't want Travis to hear. I nodded at her. 'I'll drive you home.'

#

I walked into work the next morning feeling a lot better. Patrick and Victoria were huddled in the kitchen speaking in low voices, and when I passed, Patrick stretched out a foot and kicked the door shut.

'Good morning to you too,' I muttered, sinking into my desk chair. Switching on the computer, I tried not to wonder what they were speaking about. My annoyance spiked, however. How rude, to kick the door shut like that? I summoned Bec's words from my memory. *You've gotta focus on what's most important to you, and that's being a mum.* I blew out a breath, and opened the gallery emails.

About half an hour later, Victoria sauntered into the office with a mug of coffee. She placed it down gingerly. 'Here you go, Emmy. I hope you're feeling better.'

I tried not to grimace. 'Thanks, Victoria. But I'm not sick; I'm doing just fine. And if you don't mind, no one calls me Emmy.'

'Oh right, of course,' she stammered.

'What's with secret meeting in the kitchen?' I asked, sipping my coffee. 'Anything I need to be aware of?'

'No,' she snapped. 'Everything is normal. In fact, why don't I take you over to the café for lunch? We can visit your friend Cleo.'

I gulped down a mouthful. I hadn't seen Cleo since she'd told Bec and I she was pregnant. I hadn't been avoiding the café, exactly, but… as if on cue, my belly cramped, and I thumped my mug down on the desk.

Victoria smirked, hands on hips. It was a mocking pose, but that didn't make sense. Why would she think it was a problem to go out for lunch and see Cleo?

'Fine,' I answered. 'Let's have lunch then.'

Victoria smiled sweetly and stalked away. I watched her go, my brow furrowing. What just happened?

'So you saw Cleo?'

Bec and I strolled the supermarket aisles. She wheeled a trolley with Poppy inside it. Poppy cradled the items Bec placed inside, examining the packaging.

'Yeah,' I answered, swapping my heavy basket to the other arm. 'She has morning sickness. She looked pretty pale actually.'

Bec glanced sidelong at me. 'You haven't been there since she told us she's pregnant?'

I chucked two cups of noodles into my basket. 'No.'

'You used to go there for lunch nearly every day.'

I stopped walking. 'There's been a bit going on, in case you'd forgotten,' I snapped. Poppy looked up at us with wide eyes. I swallowed. 'It's okay, Pops, no one's angry.'

We kept walking. 'I'd understand if it was hard for you to talk about it with her, that's all.'

Exasperated, I pressed my lips together. 'That wasn't even the point of my story. I wanted to tell you about Victoria, and how she suggested going there. She had this look on her face, like…'

Bec glared at me.

'What?'

'You're a bit obsessed with her,' she said quietly. She passed a box of Tiny Teddies to Poppy who shrieked with glee.

'Excuse me?'

'Let's not raise our voices in the supermarket, hey?' Bec murmured, steering the trolley into the fruit and vegetable section.

'I'm not raising my voice,' I whispered, pulling a funny face to make Poppy laugh. 'I feel like I'm being ambushed.'

'No,' Bec shook her head. 'I'm sorry if it came across that way.'

I reached for a bunch of celery, a cucumber, two red capsicums. 'Forget it.'

Bec paused for a minute, plastic bag of potatoes in hand. 'You really should.'

We collected tubs of berries and cartons of milk and queued up at the checkout. On the other side of the scanner, Victoria hooked a canvas bag of groceries over her arm and trotted through the sliding doors.

Speak of the devil.

I pulled into the garage and juggled the groceries inside. It was past five pm, but I knew immediately that the house was empty. I called out to Mark anyway. No answer. Strolling through into the kitchen, I dumped the bags on the bench and unloaded the cold items. Turning to the fridge to put them away, I froze. Beneath the fridge, something was poking out. A tail. A flat, dark, shiny tail.

'Oh Jesus fucking Christ,' I murmured, taking a slow step backwards. I fumbled for my handbag, and as quietly as I could, I withdrew my phone. I dialled Mark's number, but it went straight to voicemail. Mind racing, I stepped back again. Slowly. Quietly. I made it into the lounge room and dialled Mum's number.

'Hello, sweet–'

'Mum, there's a snake in the house.' My voice shook. I clenched the phone to my ear and backed slowly towards the front door.

'Oh shit, where is it?'

'Kitchen. Under the fridge.'

'What can you see?'

'Tail. Black. I think.'

'Lizard?'

'I don't know!'

'Could be a red-belly black.'

'Mum! What do I do?'

'Don't startle it.'

'I'm at the front door.'

'Good. Get outside if you can.'

I opened the front door. It creaked loudly. Reaching blindly for the screen door, I backed myself through it and stumbled onto the front concrete step.

'You outside?' Mum asked.

'Yeah. How do I get rid of it? Can you come get it?'

'I've never caught one before. I've never had one in the house. Usually outside you'd just move away and they'd–'

'Mum! God, please, tell me what to do. Can Dad get it?'

'Oh, he'd hopeless. A big pussycat when it comes to reptiles. One time–'

'Mum!'

'Okay, let me think. Johnno, he catches 'em.'

'Johnno?'

'At the vets, you know? The bloke with the long beard?'

'Right. Okay, can you call him? Can you send him over here?'

'Okay, love. Stay outside, stay calm.'

'Wait. What happens if Johnno comes and it's not in the kitchen?'

'Well, geez, I don't know. I guess he'll have to look for it.'

'Shit.' I hung up and dialled Mark again, leaving a message to tell him what was happening. I walked slowly down the driveway, staring at the clock on my phone. Four minutes later, a rusty old ute barrelled along the street and screeched to a stop at the curb. Johnno, beer belly hanging over a pair of khaki pants, long beard streaked with grey, climbed out of the car. In one hand he carried a long stick with a hook on the end, and in the other was a hessian sack.

'G'day love, where is the bastard?'

'In the kitchen. I saw its tail poking out from under the fridge.'

'You sure it's not a lizard?'

'Oh God, it looked like a snake to me.'

'Righto.' He swaggered up the driveway and I followed at a distance, lingering by the front door. 'Don't come inside. We don't want to scare it.'

'Okay.'

I watched through the lounge room window as Johnno made his way towards the kitchen, surprisingly light on his feet. From the window I couldn't see the fridge, and Johnno quickly disappeared from view, but I heard him yell out. 'It's a brown snake. Big bastard too!'

'Be careful!' I called back, not knowing what else to say. I didn't know much about snakes, having only seen them in the bush from a distance. But I did know that brown snakes were the ones to avoid, their venom deadly. I knew they could grow big, and when surprised they could strike. I covered my mouth and waited, peering through the glass. I heard a scraping sound and a corner of the fridge appeared. Johnno was moving the fridge to get to it. I wanted to call out again, ask him what was happening, but I didn't want to distract him.

'Got him!' he shouted suddenly, and I sprang to the door, opening it for him. The sack was bunched in his fist, unmoving.

'It's in there?'

He grinned. 'Sure is. It's bloody unusual to get one in the kitchen like that.'

'Really?'

'Oh yeah, snakes usually leave us alone unless they can help it.'

'What does that mean then?'

He shrugged, then chuckled. 'Got any enemies?'

I laughed too, but my heartbeat accelerated. I couldn't take my eyes off the sack. 'No offense, Johnno, but do you think you could leave now and take that thing with you?'

Johnno threw his head back and bellowed out a laugh. 'No worries, love.'

I smiled. 'Thanks so much for rushing over though, I really appreciate it. What do I owe you?'

Johnno shook his head and we started walking down the driveway. 'All good, mate. Don't worry about it.'

I blew out a breath. 'Thank you.' We reached his car and once he'd secured the snake, I waved him off. I wasn't in a rush to go back inside. Across the street, Mrs Nichol waved, and I headed over to her. 'Hi, Mrs Nichol.'

'Hello, Rebecca dear. Was that John from the vets just leaving?'

'Yes, we had a brown snake in the kitchen.'

She stumbled back, pressing a palm against the top of her sun hat. 'Oh my goodness, that is quite strange, isn't it?'

I squinted into the sun. 'It sure is. You haven't seen anything unusual around here?'

'No, and I'm always keeping an eye out for critters here in the garden. In all my years in this house, I've never seen a brown snake.'

I swallowed, looking up and down the street. In the distance, I could make out Mark's car. 'Okay. Well, please let us know if you see anything. If you need anything.'

'I will. Thank you. You let that husband look after you tonight, you've had a terrible fright.'

I smiled. 'Will do.'

I changed the sheets and slid into the fragrant coolness. The outside light leaked through the bedroom window where Mark was still hunting around, looking for a gap where the snake could have gotten into the house. There was nothing; no reason that we could find that would attract a deadly brown snake to our kitchen. After a light salad for dinner, I'd been so exhausted by my day that I'd showered and headed to bed.

It hadn't been a great day.

The snake. The silly argument with Bec in the supermarket. Victoria's strange behaviour and her private talk with Patrick.

Turning on my side, I reached for my Kindle and opened the book I was reading. But after a couple of pages, I gave up and switched it back off. Outside the leaves slithered against each other on the trees. Or that could have been Mark shuffling around. It wasn't quite dark yet, but even the cicadas were quiet.

I pulled the sheet up to my chin and squished my eyes shut.

The front door slammed. 'Mark?'

'Yeah, just me.'

I waited as he clomped up the hallway in his work boots. 'Find anything?'

'Nope. It's a mystery.' He frowned. 'You going to bed already?'

'I'm tired. Crappy day.'

Mark sat on the mattress and tugged off his boots. 'Yeah, I understand. Are you feeling okay though? You know, apart from the snake?'

I waved my hand. 'I'm okay. Still a bit sore but it's nothing. I just want to put today behind me.'

Mark leaned over and pressed his lips to my hair. 'I'm going to do a bit of work. Call me if you need me.'

I nodded, smiling as he flicked the fan on for me on the way out of the bedroom. And just like that, the cicadas broke into song outside the window.

Chapter 10

'Emily, a call for you,' Patrick called from my desk.

Carrying in my mug from the kitchen, I grabbed the receiver and perched on the edge of the desk. I'd been kicked off my computer while Victoria tapped away at the keyboard, Patrick dictating at her elbow.

'Hello?'

'Hey, it's me,' Bec replied. 'I just wanted to check on you. Mum said you had a brown snake in your house last night.'

'Yeah, under the fridge.' I sipped my coffee. 'The vet came and got it.'

'Shit, so you're okay?'

'I'm good.'

Victoria stopped typing; she and Patrick watched me. I smiled and stepped away, stretching the phone cord as far as it could reach. Who didn't have a cordless phone nowadays?

'Good, and I'm sorry if you thought I was having a go last night in the supermarket, I–'

'No, no,' I interrupted. 'It's all good. I'll ring you back at lunch time though, okay?'

'Ah,' Bec answered. 'Is she listening?'

'Yep. Talk to you in a bit.' I returned the phone to its cradle. When I looked up, both Victoria and Patrick were still staring.

'Did you have a snake?' Victoria asked, polished nails still hovering over the keyboard.

I narrowed my eyes at her. 'Why do you think that?'

'Well,' she stuttered. 'We heard you say the vet came and got something under your fridge, so…' Her cheeks flushed and she glanced up at Patrick for support.

'Are you okay?' Patrick asked. 'You're acting a bit…'

I made an effort to relax my body. 'A bit what?'

He shrugged. 'Bitchy.'

'Oh please, you've been calling me a bitch since primary school.' Forcing a laugh, I picked up my still-full mug and headed back to the kitchen. Victoria followed me, shutting the kitchen door behind her. My heart rate increased, but I wasn't sure why. I placed my mug down carefully and looked her in the eye.

'You don't like me, do you?' she asked. Her tone was flatter, more insistent than moments earlier when she asked me about the snake; when Patrick was nearby, listening.

'What?' I tried to smile, but her eyes were cold. The room around me seemed to close in, walls pressing up against my ribcage.

Victoria stepped closer, her heels clicking on the floor. 'I have tried to be nice to you, Emily. You have been rude and mean to me ever since I started here.' Her voice had deepened significantly; it had a creepy quality to it that made me swallow hard. I felt small under her piercing gaze and I straightened my spine, forcing myself to make eye contact.

'I'm sorry if you feel that way, Victoria, I–'

'Don't bother lying to me,' she snarled, her top lip curling. 'I know. I *know.*'

My breath caught in my throat. There was nothing I could say to her in that moment; my mind had been wiped clean. She towered over me, her painted face looming like a scary plastic doll's. I tried not to shrink away, but I couldn't help leaning back. She was a different person to the one who made me coffee in the morning and giggled with Patrick. She was cold and threatening, and, perhaps irrationally, I felt a bit frightened.

'Enough girl talk,' Patrick bellowed. I jumped, the spell broken by his familiar voice. Victoria froze then slowly shook her head, and the threatening mask fell away.

'You're the boss,' she called back, her voice an octave higher, girlish, flirtatious. She ran a hand through her hair, turning on her heel. At the door, she glanced at me over her shoulder. 'By the way, Emily, I'm so sorry to hear you're having trouble at home. You've got to watch out for those snakes, especially the brown ones. They're quite venomous, you know.'

I sagged against the bench. Left alone in the kitchen, I closed my eyes a moment. My body was shaking and I chastised myself. Victoria was a bitch, but bitches were everywhere. And she was right on one point; I hadn't treated her very nicely. But I'd been at the gallery longer, and I was good at my job. Ever since she'd arrived, Patrick had been bewitched by her, and if they were sleeping together, then what hope did I have? If she was determined to take over my job, then how could I stop her?

I took some deep breaths, willing myself to calm down. How did she do that to me? I didn't consider myself a pushover, but she had shaken me up. Pouring my coffee down the sink, I replayed the scene, and it was then that I remembered her comment about the snake. *Trouble at home. Brown snake.* How did she know it was a brown snake?

At home I jumped on the exercise bike and pedalled hard. I wanted to burn away the discomforting thoughts about my argument with Victoria. In my workout pants, t-shirt soaked with sweat, I rode in the warm afternoon breeze, trying to remember how the conversation went, trying *not* to think about it.

Mark came home and found me slumped over the handlebars, heaving in breaths, legs relentlessly pumping. He grabbed my hips to still them and I relented, sliding off the bike.

'Shit, honey, should you be doing that?'

I waved a hand while I caught my breath. 'I'm okay.'

'If you say you had a bad day again, then–'

'Then what?'

'Then I'd have to ask you if the job is worth it.'

I straightened my shoulders. 'So I just let her take it?'

'See, I knew you'd say that.' Mark turned away, walking towards the kitchen. I followed, found him bending into the fridge to pull out a beer. 'It's just a job, not a fight to the death. If you're going to be unhappy, then just quit.'

'So that's how much your job means to you? If someone you worked with made you uncomfortable, if they bullied you, then you'd just forget the job and leave?'

Mark swigged, burped. 'Yep.' He raised the bottle again, hesitated. 'What do you mean, bullied?'

I leaned against the bench and weighed my options. If I repeated the conversation to Mark would it sound petty and ridiculous? Or would I be able to portray the uneasiness I felt? I decided to go for it; he was my husband after all.

'She cornered me in the kitchen today and said she knew I didn't like her, and that she knows I've been having trouble at home.'

Mark raised his eyebrows, waited.

'She knew about the snake.' I paused. 'Although Bec did call and they overheard, but she knew it was a brown snake. She told me to watch out for them because they're venomous.'

Slowly Mark put down his beer. 'You think she planted a brown snake under our fridge?'

'No!' I spluttered. 'No. But how did she know it was a brown snake? She was very confrontational about the whole thing, and I can't explain it, she made me nervous.' I shook my head, knowing that I wouldn't be able to convey how I felt, and regretting that I had chosen to tell him. 'I don't know. I felt really uncomfortable.'

'Maybe she has a point.'

'Great, you're defending her.'

Mark sighed. 'I'm not defending her, but you *don't* like her. Do you?'

'I've tried, Mark. But there's something about her that's… off, I can't explain it.'

He pulled me against his chest, kissed my sweaty forehead. 'There are more important things for you to think about, honey. Remember?'

I nodded against him. 'Bec says that too.'

'Then don't forget it. It's just a job, but what we're trying to do is for *us*. Our lives together.'

'A family.'

'A family. She's not a part of that. She's not important.'

I slept fitfully, unable to switch off the details of the day. When I reached out for Mark in the early hours, I found him turned away from me, clinging to the edge of the mattress. Tracing my fingers over his bare shoulder blades, I eased him back against my body, holding him close. Could the stress over trying for a baby justify my unease around Victoria? Was I seeing things that weren't really there? Even since the laparoscopy, I hadn't turned my life upside down with special diets and hours of research, but maybe that was the problem? Maybe if I focused all my attention on trying to get pregnant, I wouldn't be putting so much emphasis on my job. Because when it came down to it, Mark and Bec were right. It was just a job, and family was a lifetime commitment.

I slipped out of bed and padded out into the kitchen. Filling a glass with water, I sat at the table and flicked on my laptop. We hadn't received a date for a follow-up appointment with Dr Kemp yet. Soon, I would chase that up. But for now, it was time to research. Finally, after all these months – month after month after month – I was going to arm myself with information.

Hours later, the early morning breeze tickled my face.

I stared through the open door out into the backyard, at the lightening sky and groups of birds happily taking flight. Clouds of insects hovered over the dewy grass. In the bushes by the fence, an echidna snuffled through the dirt. Branches swayed melodically in the pale yellow morning.

All around me, signs of life.

On my computer, tales of woe.

Regret clawed at my throat. I shouldn't have read their stories, I knew I shouldn't have. And now the words were imprinted on my brain. *Why can't I get pregnant? My partner and I never use protection… and we've never had a close call. I've tried everything, and nothing has worked.* The reassuring stories even, from older women who were never able to conceive but still led happy lives, added the stamp of despair in my mind. Why did I delve into this world, this reality? I knew the stories were out there, I knew there would be countless tips and positions and diets to try. And I knew when Mark and I first started trying that I didn't want to be one of *those* women, obsessing over every little thing.

But I'd crossed the line tonight. I felt involved now. Like I needed to take a proactive approach in my mission to conceive. And that I had to report my efforts to these strange women out there who had my back.

I stretched, rubbing fingers into my gritty eyes. Mark would be getting up soon and I had to hide my nocturnal activities. After our conversation yesterday, I didn't want him to worry about me further. I had to handle this myself – this day job and this bigger, life-changing job of making a baby.

#

I walked into the office and a swell of voices. Patrick, Victoria and a third familiar voice. *Cleo.* Hair tied off her face, and the subtle curve of her belly under her apron. I hesitated in the doorway. Spread across the desk, an array of colourful muffins and coffee cups. And Victoria, reaching over to gingerly touch Cleo's stomach. A giggle, a soft squeal, and then they saw me.

'Emily!' Victoria gushed. 'Cleo brought us breakfast!'

I frowned, her words yesterday still fresh. Yet here was that damn mask again, and she was making nice in front of the others. Forcing a smile, I hugged Cleo and thanked her.

'It was Victoria really,' Cleo said. 'She wanted to treat you.'

'And catch up with the glowing mum-to-be,' Victoria chipped in.

'Glowing, ha.' Cleo swiped a hand over her shiny forehead. 'Glowing with sweat maybe.'

'You feel okay?' I asked, reaching for a coffee cup. I willed the caffeine to enter my bloodstream quickly as I took a sip.

Cleo shrugged. 'Yeah, I feel pretty good. Just tired.' Her hand traced a circle over her abdomen and I tried not to watch, but the movement was hypnotic and I found myself reliving the stories I'd read last night – especially the rage of one woman seeing expectant mothers stroke their bellies in such a way. *Do they have to constantly draw attention to it? Don't they know that some women can't have kids or do they just not care?*

Clearing my throat, I gave Cleo a slight squeeze. 'I'll see you soon.' I moved quietly away. Patrick sauntered off with coffee and a muffin until it was just Victoria, bailing Cleo up with stories about motherhood. Swallowing hard, I busied myself with the day's tasks. *It's just a job. Just get through the day.*

I ducked home at lunch time, something I usually only did when I didn't want to go to Cleo's, and couldn't bear to sit in the gallery kitchen to eat my lunch. Today certainly qualified as one of those days where I just needed to have a few minutes alone in the privacy of my own home.

Stripping down to my underwear, I sat on the floor in front of the air conditioner with a bowl of cherries and a bottle of water, and I tried not to think. I tried not to remember the night before, reading all those stories, feeling the emotional pain of those people I didn't even know. And Cleo, tracing circles on her belly, a belly barely rounded by the tiny foetus inside her. And Victoria, with her fake smile and high-pitched voice, and obsession with talking about motherhood.

When I returned to work, Patrick and Victoria were chatting to a local artist, Mr Sa. I waved to him, moving through into the office, where I dumped my bag and sank down in front of the computer. There, on the screen, was Mark's face. I frowned, confused, and clicked the mouse. It was Mark's Facebook page, a photo album titled 'Holidays'. Sitting back in my chair, I thought about it. Was it Patrick or Victoria who was looking at Mark's Facebook photos? It made no sense for Patrick to do so... there was no conceivable reason I could come up with as to why Patrick would feel the need to do that... on the office computer instead of his own. Which meant Victoria had been looking at my husband. She was checking out my husband.

I managed to wait until she'd returned to the office, and thankfully she returned without Patrick. Mark's page was still on the screen and I pointed at it without a word. I studied her carefully as she looked at the computer, I saw her stiffen, I saw the mask go up. When she turned to me, a careful smile was painted on her face, an innocent smile.

'That's your gorgeous husband,' she said with a shrug and an infuriating giggle.

'Yes it is, and why would you be looking at pictures of him?'

Her brow furrowed, and irritation coursed through me. 'What do you mean?'

'This was on the screen when I came in, and I wasn't looking at it.'

She chuckled. 'Well, you must have been–'

I stood up. 'Can you please just stop with the crap, Victoria?'

Patrick interrupted, sauntering in and nodding at both of us. 'What kind of work do you call this?'

Victoria tossed her hair and shot him a dazzling smile. 'Girl talk is very important work, Pat, trust me.'

Patrick laughed as he headed into his office.

I waited, heart thumping, as she turned back to me. It seemed to happen in slow motion, and I didn't know who I would find when she faced me. But she was still smiling, and with a condescending tilt of her head, she walked away without saying anything.

I drove home through a haze of smoke Bec assured me

was not a concern. The summers were frequently like this around here, smoke drifting into town from small fires often caused by lightning strikes. Some spread and became a problem, but others were quickly forgotten as they were put out and the smoke dissipated. It had become a habit to check in with Bec or Travis when there was smoke; they kept up to date on what was happening in our area.

The afternoon was eerie and yellow, like an old sepia-toned photograph. Pulling into the garage, I spotted a large package on our front doorstep. Switching on the air con in the sweltering house, I made my way to the front door to collect the parcel. There was no address on the label, so I tore into the brown wrapping paper. On the box underneath was a picture of a baby's bouncing chair, decorated with brightly-coloured tropical fish. Frowning, I carried the box into the house and set it by the front door. Why on earth would Mark buy such a thing when we weren't even pregnant? I certainly wouldn't.

I spent the next hour talking to Bec, who was at home clearing scrub from around the farmhouse. She told me about the fire nearby, that although it wasn't a problem she was on alert, watching the weather. She got into my head, and after I hung up, I went outside in my old cut-offs and singlet to search the perimeter of the house. Our townhouse was relatively clear, with only a small backyard and Mark's shed taking up space. There certainly wasn't any scrub to worry about; however, I grabbed my shears and trimmed back the trees, tidying up the branches and dead leaves. I watered everything down, setting up the sprinkler to soak the dry grass and the parched trunks. Working off my shitty day with physical labour.

When I eventually headed back inside, wet grass sticking to my thongs and bare legs, Mark had unboxed the baby bouncing chair and was staring quizzically at it.

'You bought this?' he asked by way of greeting.

'No.' I kicked off my thongs and tiptoed over towards him. 'Didn't you?'

'No.' He scrunched up the brown paper in his fists.

'Then why did you take it out? They probably sent it to the wrong person.'

'How? You bought anything else from these people?' He looked at the label. '*Bubba Dreams.*' He snorted. 'Would you buy anything from a shop called *Bubba Dreams?*'

I couldn't help but join in his laughter. 'No, bubba. I would not shop at *Bubba Dreams.*'

He grinned. 'Why are you all wet?'

'Was chatting to Bec. She was clearing around the farmhouse to get ready for this heatwave we're supposed to get. So I've pruned and watered everything down.'

'Geez honey, we'll be fine here, we're smack bang in the middle of town.'

'Yeah, I know.' I thought of telling him about today, about Victoria looking at him online, but kept quiet. Instead I fingered the soft fabric of the bouncing chair, and asked, 'so who do you think sent us this?'

'Well, there's only one person who knows we're trying.' Mark raised his eyebrows and pelted the brown paper towards the rubbish bin. He missed.

'No, she wouldn't.'

'You sure?'

I texted Bec, and moments later, when she had replied that she hadn't ordered us any gifts, I showed Mark the screen. He shrugged.

Returning his shrug, I wrestled the chair back into the box. Padding barefoot up the hallway, I shoved the box into the spare room and shut the door.

#

I woke to the sound of screaming. Jumping out of bed, Mark and I exchanged worried glances and began to pull on any items of clothes we could find. We ran to the front of the house. The sun blinded me as I wrenched the door open, and I stumbled sightless down the front steps. Across the street, in the driveway of Mrs Nichol's house, a middle-aged woman was bent double, hands wrapped across her head.

Mr Cork from next door was already there, hovering behind her, fingers fluttering like useless moths. As he saw us coming he visibly sagged, and met us by the front fence. 'I can't get her to say what's wrong.'

As the woman slowly straightened, I recognised her. Mrs Nichol's daughter. 'Katrina?'

She turned wide eyes on to me. 'Horrible,' she whispered. 'Horrible.'

Chapter 11

I grabbed Katrina by the shoulders. 'What's happened?'
'It's Mum. Oh God, *Mum*.'

Mark ran towards the house and I followed, climbing the front concrete steps and peering into the dim interior. There was nothing out of place in the lounge room. Recliner with a crocheted rug folded neatly on the back, china cabinet full of matching dinner sets, ancient TV gathering dust. Through to the kitchen, the makings of a meal were spread across the bench top. I headed that way, Mark on my heels. As I got closer, I covered my nose. I couldn't be sure if it was the sliced vegetables on the chopping board that smelled rancid, or if it was something else. Stepping over the threshold into the kitchen, the smell grew stronger and I tried not to gag. Mark groaned, and I followed his gaze.

Mrs Nichol sat slumped against the fridge, grey-faced and eyes open. There was a profound stillness to her, an emptiness, her face devoid of any expression.

It was clear she was dead.

A vegetable knife lay in her lap, one hand resting on the handle. Her stockinged feet stuck straight out in front, and through the nylon I could see her toenails were painted red.

Stepping backwards from the room, I walked purposefully back towards the front door; a glowing beacon lit with morning sun.

Outside, other neighbours had gathered around Katrina, who sat on the manicured lawn with her head in her hands. I went to her, dropping to my haunches and touching her shoulder. 'Was she sick?'

Katrina's eyes were haunted as they locked on to mine. 'You know she wasn't. She was fine.'

'But…' I tried to think of something to say but my brain felt scrambled. 'How old was she though? I mean…'

'She was old but she wasn't sick,' Katrina snapped, lowering her head again.

I sank down next to her on the grass. Mark joined us, and together we waited for emergency services.

#

'I've never seen a dead body before, it was really horrible.'

That Sunday, we sat at my parents' kitchen table nursing cold drinks after our barbecue lunch. Poppy had gone down for a nap so the six adults sat in the air conditioning and out of the smoke haze, finally able to talk about Mrs Nichol.

'She had a good innings, love,' Dad said, laying a calloused hand on my arm. 'And she got to go at home, without any fuss. That's how she would've wanted it.'

'Yeah, I know, but Katrina said she wasn't sick, I don't

understand how she can just die like that.'

'At that age, the body's wearing out,' Mum countered. 'She *was* in her eighties.'

'Right,' I nodded. But Katrina's comments haunted me. And Mrs Nichol had seemed so healthy for a woman in her eighties.

'You've had a shock seeing her like that.' Mum refilled my glass of ice water.

I looked over at Mark, who sat quietly. He too had seen her like that, caught that whiff of death that hung heavy in her kitchen. We hadn't talked much about it since it happened, the images were too awful. We hadn't talked about much at all in the last couple of days, in fact, throwing ourselves into our work and night time routines. Thankfully, Victoria had kept that fake smiling mask in place ever since I'd caught her looking at Mark online.

'She used to get us mixed up, remember?' Bec swigged her beer and grinned. 'I saw her in the supermarket only last week and it was "Hello, Emily dear."'

I laughed. 'Yeah, I was always "Rebecca dear".'

'Sweet woman,' Mum smiled.

We spoke of the fire threat then, with a different fire sparking overnight in parkland only twenty kilometres away. The smoke drifted down over us from the hills, blurring the landscape and tickling our throats. Bec and Travis had received an alert about the fire but had not gone out to fight it; according to Travis the blaze was small and it was more useful to monitor the situation from home.

'Dad, you should probably get rid of that scrub on the south boundary,' Bec said.

Dad chuckled. 'Oh come on, love, we've never had a

problem before. We're always careful, you know that.'

Bec drained her beer. 'Yeah, but you're also a stubborn bastard. I know you; if you're under threat you're likely to stay put and try to fight it.'

'Bloody oath I would, we built this house. Raised you girls in this house.'

'But you don't have the training, Dad.'

'Don't get up on your high horse. You think I don't know a thing or two about fires? I've lived in the country my whole life.'

Bec sighed. 'Righto.'

I glanced across at Dad. His lips had hardened into a white line, and he rapped his knuckles on the table. He had always been tough, but lately I'd noticed a new softness to him, a vulnerability that probably came with age. As a grandpa to Poppy, I'd seen the playful side that I hadn't seen as much when Bec and I were growing up. He was always working; too busy to play. Now I scrutinised his face, and noticed new lines etched into his skin. And something in my chest went *bang*… I needed to give him another chance to be a grandpa. I wanted desperately for him to see me have a child, to give *both* my parents that moment of seeing their other daughter give birth.

I'd finally stopped bleeding a couple of days ago, my insides had healed. I had to keep trying, keep fighting for the family Mark and I wanted. Mrs Nichol's death had lit a fire under me; it was a reminder that we could all go at any time.

Across the table I caught Mum's eye and quickly looked away. After that day at our place, I knew she could sense something, and with my heart rate winding up and emotion clogging my chest, I didn't want to give in and tell her what was going on.

Instead I sat very quietly while Dad and Bec argued about their fire plans, staring at the condensation weeping down my glass and pooling on the coaster.

I went back to Bec's place for a late drink, while Mark went home to work in the shed. Sitting on the veranda, I stretched out my bare legs and stared out over the hazy paddocks.

'I can rely on you, right? If we decide to go and fight, you could stay here with Poppy?' Bec pinned me with her gaze. Her top was askew from where Poppy leant against her, playing with Barbies. I watched the perfectly dipped plastic figures prance across the veranda boards, and the little fingers that controlled them.

'Yeah, or you could just bring her into our place. It's safer in town anyway.'

'We're not under threat here,' Bec snapped. 'If anyone is, it's Mum and Dad.'

'The wind can change the fire's direction in a second, you know that,' I shot back.

Travis stood abruptly from the veranda step. 'I know girl talk when I hear it.' He marched across the backyard, unwinding the hose to water the plants. Poppy ran after her dad, one doll still clutched in her fist.

'Alberton not's that big,' I continued. 'If the fire spots or something then *either* you or Mum and Dad could come under threat. Just because it's closer to Mum and Dad's now doesn't mean anything. I think it's safest to bring Poppy to our place.'

Bec sat forward. 'Safest? Travis and I are trained firefighters.'

'Yes, I know,' I murmured.

Bec stood and walked inside and I followed her. Inside it was dark, messy, and hot. She had flung open the fridge and was pulling out the makings of a salad. A lettuce rolled across the bench and dropped into the sink. I watched her, confused and disappointed. I'd wanted to talk to her alone for a while, to tell her about Victoria and to vent about the tension between me and Mark. But she was distracted by this fire, and so now it was my job to be there for her.

'You know, Dad won't leave no matter what. Mum will stay there too, to help him, and if I just want my daughter to stay here where it's normal, with all her toys and her own bed–'

'Okay, I get it. But it's normal at my place too. She's there all the time. It could be like a holiday, a sleepover while her mum and dad–'

'It's not a holiday, and you don't know what it's like.'

I frowned. Bec rarely got so worked up about things. 'Then quit if you get so stressed about it.'

'Christ, it's not that! I'm trying to do the best for my child. I'm trying to work and protect her and everyone has a fucking opinion about how I should be doing it.' She slammed a capsicum on a chopping board and drove a knife into it.

I crossed my arms and swallowed. 'And I don't get an opinion as her aunty? Besides, I wasn't *telling you what to do*. And I've got my own shit going on, believe it or not, so you having a go at me is really unfair.'

Bec raked her fingers through her hair. 'Em, just stop talking. You're not a parent; you don't understand.'

Heat thumped through my body, pulsated in my temples. Bec flushed bright red, and her mouth gaped open as she realised what she'd said. Around me the room receded, shrinking until it was just the two of us. My breath halted, my fingers twitched, and I wanted nothing more than to run. So I did; first backing out of the room, then snatching my bag and stalking to the front door. Bec didn't follow.

Clattering down the veranda steps, I fumbled blindly through my bag for my keys. The evening was warm and still, like a storm was coming, but I barely noticed as I dove into the car and gunned the engine. Hearing those words had caused a feeling like panic to squeeze the air from my chest. My face was burning with anger or shame, I couldn't tell. I had to get away.

I sped down the driveway, dust obscuring the windscreen, and as I turned to head home my brain clicked into gear, that innate part of my country self that knew I had to slow down, to watch out for roos and wombats. But my eyes were filling up, and after a couple of minutes I pulled the car over and switched off the engine. I sucked in a lungful of air, and deep inside my gut, a knot loosened and finally let go. Doubling over the steering wheel, I howled. My mouth opened wide, eager to spill out everything I felt. Frustration. Anger. Humiliation. Fear.

I let it all go, screaming out all these months of trying and failing.

Once I felt exhausted, my throat burning and eyes swollen, I pressed my forehead against the steering wheel and took some deep, shuddering breaths. Sweat had collected under my arms and I lifted them, wrapping them over the wheel. Now that I had quieted, I could hear my phone's ringtone drifting from my bag on the passenger seat. I pulled it out. Seeing Bec's name I didn't answer, but opened my messages to read a text from her.

I'm sorry. Please come back so we can talk.

I realised then what I felt. *Betrayal.* She was the only person who knew our secret, and she had thrown it in my face. Another message pinged through.

I'm just angry with Dad, not you. I'm so sorry.

Frowning, I closed my eyes. I didn't want to go back and listen to her explanations; I wanted to go home and forget what she'd said. I had to let it go, I knew that. Besides Mark, she was my ally, my best friend, and she knew me in a way Mark couldn't.

Blowing out a long breath, I shook my head as she texted again.

Are you okay?

Finally, I responded, my thumbs clumsy.

I'll talk to you tomorrow.

At home, I lit the candles in the bedroom after soaking in a long bath and finding my favourite lingerie. I read for a while, waiting for Mark to join me, but when he didn't, I slipped on my dressing gown and headed out to the shed. The night was cool, with a slight smokiness on the breeze. The shed door squealed open and I stepped into the gloomy interior. Mark lay sprawled on his tattered recliner, a coil of smoke streaming from between his fingers. The sweet tang of pot hit my nostrils and my mouth dropped open. I could count on one hand the number of times Mark and I had smoked weed together, and as far as I knew, he never smoked it alone out here in his shed.

He looked up as I approached, eyes half-open. 'Hey, honey.'

'What the fuck are you doing?' I snapped, unable to stop myself. Shivering, I wrapped my arms across my middle. 'Is this what you do when you come out to the shed to work on the cot? You sit here and smoke a joint like some pot head?'

He sighed, the sound rattling out from deep in his chest. 'No, Em, of course not.'

I gestured to his hand with a shake of my head. 'Then what are you doing?'

He sat up and patted the arm of the recliner. I kept standing. I'd driven the long way home tonight to compose myself and arrived home determined to shrug off Bec's comment and keep trying, and now this?

'It's just lately,' Mark murmured. 'Lately, I don't know, the tests and the operation, and then the pressure when we do have sex. And I know we said we wouldn't pressure ourselves, but how can it not be pressure? Then we saw Mrs Nichol over there and still it's the sex schedule because we have to keep trying and keep trying, and… I don't know if I can handle it.'

I did sit then, clasping his hand. 'What are you saying? You don't want to try anymore?'

He squashed the butt on the top of an empty beer can. 'I think we should take a break.'

'A break…' My stomach began to hurt, a sharp pain that threatened to take my breath away.

'Let's just forget about it for a while, can we? Please?'

I released his hand and stood on shaking legs. The concrete floor was gritty under my bare feet. Wood shavings, dirt, dust, cobwebs and the pungent smoke made me light-headed. I walked towards the door, passing the sheet-covered shape of the half-finished cot. I'd thought he kept it covered because he didn't want me to see it before it was finished, but now I wondered if he covered it for his own benefit, if he'd been working on it at all. All those nights he'd come out here to "work on the cot" could have been his way of escaping the pressure of our situation. And was it my fault? Was *I* the one pressuring him? Because it was something we both wanted, wasn't it? And if not, why would he pretend it was?

In the bedroom I blew out the candles and crawled into bed. Mark hadn't followed me inside, even though I hadn't answered his question. I wondered what he was doing, if he would even remember our conversation in the morning. Curling into a ball, I wrapped my hands across my stomach and squeezed my eyes shut. When had his feelings changed? Why so suddenly? What was I supposed to do now?

My throat burned. I told myself it was because of the smoke, and had nothing to do with the tears dripping onto my pillow.

#

I slipped out of bed before six, glancing at Mark in the dark. He didn't stir; lips puffing out the even breaths of heavy sleep. Throwing on shorts and a t-shirt, tying up my hair, I grabbed my beach bag from the hallway and threw a few supplies in it. Sunscreen, hat, bottled water, snacks, and a couple of paperbacks I hadn't gotten around to reading yet. I texted Patrick as I backed out of the garage, telling him I wouldn't be at work before switching off my phone. What was the point of work anyway? My life had been turned upside down so suddenly by the other half of this partnership who had decided he'd had enough, and my dear sister stabbing me where she knew it would hurt the most. Maybe talking to them in the light of day would help things, maybe Mark would take it back… maybe Mark had just been tired, stoned, frustrated, and the sun shining would clear his head and make things right again… I didn't know. All I knew was my stomach hurt with the very real possibility that there'd never be a baby in it because my husband didn't want to try anymore, and my sister didn't have my back.

I drove the familiar getaway road to the beach. I climbed out into the car park; there were a few cars parked nearby but it wasn't busy for an early mid-summer morning. Trudging along the track, I inhaled the salt air and felt my muscles loosen, my stomach finally unclench. When the ocean appeared before me, I stopped for a second, appreciating the cool salt air combing its fingers through my hair, gently shifting my clothes. Surfers dotted the horizon, sitting on their boards and waiting. I knew how they felt. The compulsion to get up early and search for something they loved, only to sit there, waiting, understanding it may not come.

Finding a spot in full sun, I spread my towel. Stretching out, I closed my eyes and the sun through my eyelids coloured my world pink, the breeze tickling my bare legs. Finally I felt able to relax, and the slight guilt I had over missing a day's work dissipated. I knew I should text Mark, tell him where I was, but I didn't want to confront that yet. So I stayed still, listening to the roar of the waves, the squawk of seagulls in the distance.

I woke, parched, gasping for water. Rolling over towards my bag, I groped for it, my skin stinging. I'd been well and truly baked by the sun. Swearing, I gulped down water, yanking the towel out from under my body as I did so. I had to get out of here. The sun, high overhead, belted down its early afternoon rays. I'd been here for hours, and a bubble of panic popped in my belly. I'd turned my phone off; I'd shut out the world. I'd escaped for almost half a day, but I didn't feel better.

In the car I switched on my phone.

Mark: *I woke up and you'd gone. Why is your phone off? We should talk about last night.*

Patrick: *See you tomorrow then.*

Mark: *Are you ok?*

Bec: *You're not at work today? Was going to meet you for lunch.*

Mark: *Please turn your phone on.*

Bec: *Mark said you left early this morning. I'm worried about you. Please call me.*

Mark: *I love you.*

Ignoring the two voicemail notifications, I tossed the phone onto the passenger seat and started the engine. At 3pm, Mark would surely be at work, but I'd find him, make things right again. Then I'd deal with Bec, sort things out.

I blasted the air conditioning onto my flushed face. In

the rear view mirror, a cherry-coloured forehead reflected back. *Idiot.* Taking the curves with ease, I ran through what I'd say to Mark, how I'd bring up last night, or if he'd beat me to it. We didn't fight; we always talked things out before they became a problem. But this baby was becoming a bit of a problem, an obstacle between us that was beginning to threaten who we were as a couple, or who I thought we were.

As I rounded a corner, I swerved to avoid a Landcruiser parked halfway across the road. 'Move over, dickhead,' I mumbled, hitting the accelerator. The trees flashed by in a blur of green and brown as I approached the highway that headed to home, but the blast of a horn from behind caused me to tap my brakes and glance into the mirror. The Landcruiser. I frowned, easing my foot onto the brake as behind me the driver flashed their lights and blared the horn again. The trees were thick here; there was no place to pull over to let him pass. But I crossed the left line and tried to slow the car as the Landcruiser bore down. Gravel sprayed under my wheels, and clenching my teeth, I prayed the tyres would hold. 'Arsehole!' I screamed.

But it was too late.

The Landcruiser's bull bar loomed large in the rear view mirror. A bump from behind. The wheels spun out. Trees loomed.

Then the crunch of metal into wood.

Shattering glass.

Thump of airbag into my face.

Silence.

Silence so loud it hurt.

A car door slamming.

Hands cupped against a broken window.

Blonde hair.

A familiar giggle. 'Whoops.'

Pain hit. Fast and hard. I wanted to claw away the airbag, but I couldn't move. I struggled to peer into the face at the window, the cupped hands. But the person was gone.

I was alone.

Tasting blood, I opened my mouth and screamed.

Chapter 12

Footsteps. Voices.
'Can you hear me? Open your eyes.'
Flashing lights. Movement. Silhouettes. Faces.
'Hold her head still.'
'Careful with the legs.'
'Hello? Ma'am? Can you hear me?'

Emily.
Emily.
My name is Emily.
I'm sunburnt. The sun has scorched my face raw, but I stay on the sand anyway, hypnotised by the wash of waves, the scrape of sand under my heels. Stretching out, I cup my chin in my palm and stare as far out as I can, searching for surfers, for boats, for any sign of life on the horizon. Nothing. I'm totally alone here, and the sun has gone, just like that. The night wind whips off the ocean with such force I have to cover my face. It's cold. I'm

shivering. Where did I park the car? How do I find my way home?

'Emily?'

I'm not on the beach. I remember now. The crash. The whip-crack pain against my chest, my face. And the other face… looking at me through the window.

'Emily?'

I pried my eyes apart. Loosening a scream, I opened my mouth, but something sticky was covering it. I swatted at it, finding an oxygen mask.

'Calm down, Emily. You're at the hospital.'

I tried to shake my head, but couldn't move it. Pain bloomed, but I couldn't pinpoint it. Panic swelled in my belly and I gasped for my voice. 'Please. I can't move.'

'Emily, stay calm. We need to keep you still until we know what injuries you might have. Please try and stay calm.'

'My husband,' I whispered. 'My husband. Can you call him?'

'Yes, of course. Don't worry now. I'm giving you something to help you relax, okay?'

The wheels clickety clacking.
White. White. White.
Bright lights.
A puff of cool air.
A long white tunnel.
My feet are cold.
Whoosh. Clickety clack.
A train on the tracks.

'Oh, Christ, Em.'

My eyes shot open and took in Mark's face, looming over me. He smelt of sawdust and sunscreen and instantly my body relaxed.

'Honey,' he whispered, palms on my face. 'What happened?'

'The car…'

He shook his head and his lips tightened. 'I know, I know, but how? What *happened*, Em?'

My eyes filled as I remembered the face peering in at the window. The blonde hair, so familiar. And I knew exactly who it was. But *why* would Victoria want to hurt me? And how could I tell Mark? I had to try, didn't I? He was my husband; he would have to believe me. But I had just smashed our car into trees. The airbag had exploded in my face. Could I really trust what I had seen? What I *thought* I had seen?

'I was run off the road,' I answered.

Mark wiped beneath my eyes with his thumbs. 'Are you serious?'

'A car bumped into me from behind and I lost control in the gravel,' I continued.

'Em,' Mark whispered. 'Are you sure? You've had a shock.'

Irritation heated my cheeks. 'It bumped me. I tried to steer out of the gravel but I couldn't. It was too fast.'

'You were speeding?'

'No! I'd been to the beach, and–'

'Yeah, I know. You took off without telling me, but I figured out that's where you'd go.'

'I'm sorry, but I needed a day off. I didn't want to think

about anything…' My eyes stung again and I blinked the tears away.

'I'm sorry that I upset you last night, Em. But I always want to be honest with you. We're a team, you and me. We have to work together.' Mark kissed my forehead, ran his hands over my cheeks.

'I don't know if I can handle this,' I whispered.

'We'll handle it together,' Mark whispered back. 'I promise.'

I swallowed. 'Then why don't you believe me about the car?'

Mark stepped back, lowering himself into a nearby chair. 'It's not that I don't believe you. But things have been crazy lately, with your work and Mrs Nichol… Bec told me what happened last night and then I make it worse by… Look, maybe it was some arsehole getting too close to try and overtake and you just thought that…' Mark ran his hands through his hair. 'It doesn't matter. None of this matters.'

I watched Mark carefully. His face was pale, and his Adam's apple worked as he swallowed hard. 'Are you okay?'

He chuckled. 'Trust you to ask *me* if I'm okay. As long as you're okay then I'm okay.'

'Am I okay?'

Mark stood again, leaning over me to stroke my hair. 'Yes, honey, you're okay. They gave you an MRI and some X-rays, do you remember?'

'Not really.'

'You have a broken leg, and your chest is bruised from the seat belt.'

'It hurts to breathe.'

'Yeah. But you're going to be fine.'

Lifting my head gingerly, I peered towards the end of the bed. My left leg was in a plaster cast, propped up on pillows. I didn't remember them doing that, I didn't remember much at all. 'What about the car?'

He blew out a breath. 'The car's totalled.'

I gulped down a sob. 'Oh no, Mark–'

Mark held a finger to my lips. 'Listen, I've got my work car, and Bec and your parents are close by. We'll manage.'

'We can't afford another car.'

'We'll manage,' Mark repeated. 'We've got insurance. You just need to rest, honey. Are you in pain?'

I thought about it. I hadn't noticed the pain ever since I'd woken up and found Mark in the room. Now, however, the throb in my leg made itself known. 'My leg hurts, but it's not so bad.'

'You're on some hardcore shit. Just relax now.'

Mark continued stroking my hair and I let my eyelids drift closed. But I couldn't relax, not completely. Behind my eyes, fear scratched a sharp fingernail against my brain. Something was very wrong, I could feel it. But I wasn't sure if it was something wrong with me… Was I going crazy, looking for a threat when there wasn't one? Or was Victoria really responsible for this? And why would that be? What could she possibly want? My husband?

By the time I was alone it was late at night. The room was lit only by a light above my bed, dim but annoying. I turned my head against the pillow, but my eyes swam, the drug haze making me dizzy.

Mum and Dad had visited, with a sheepish Bec not

long after, but I hadn't mentioned Victoria to them. What was the point if my own husband didn't even believe me? I couldn't work out a strategy to deal with this, but I knew I would have to. My mind couldn't focus; the drugs and the pain were muddling my thoughts. Nothing seemed practical and easy; common sense felt just beyond my reach, too confusing, too vast to approach.

There was no way to keep time, and the night stretched endlessly ahead. I was alone in the room; a bed across from me sat starched white and empty. The night was punctuated only by the nurses' visits, to lift me on and off the bedpan, administer more painkillers, and offer me food. I nibbled on sandwiches, unable to figure out what the fillings were between the cold, slightly wet bread. The nurse had pulled a tray across the bed so I could reach my water and I sipped at it gratefully, cooling my sore throat. I watched the window for traces of light around the blinds, but every time I looked there seemed to be just solid darkness. Willing myself to sleep, I made my body still, trying desperately to ignore the dull thump of pain in my lower leg. I was stuck on my back, unable to turn onto either side. After what felt like hours, my back stiffened, and the urge to curl up on my side began to consume me.

The window… still dark.

Thinking of the crash, I tried to work a way around having only one car. It was only then I realised there was no way for me to live my normal life with a broken leg. How could I work? Would I be able to go to work at all? *Is that why Victoria did this, to steal my job? What kind of nut job cares about an assistant's job at a tiny country art gallery?*

The window. Milky light at the edges of the blinds. Thank

God. I needed to get out of here. I needed to go home and talk to Mark, figure out some plans. I'd never had a broken leg, or any broken bone before. I had no idea what to expect.

#

'These crutches hurt my pits.'

Mark smiled as we edged across the car park. Each agonising step brought us closer to Mark's ute, but sent a ripple of pain across my bruised chest. 'Gotta practise, honey. You'll need them for weeks.'

I grunted. 'So I've got to talk to Patrick today, okay? I was thinking that with one car, it might be tricky but if you dropped me off in the mornings, maybe Mum could pick me up in the afternoons and drop me home?'

Mark stopped and glared. 'You're kidding, right?'

Gripping the handles on the crutches, I returned his stare. 'I have to go to work.'

'No, you don't, and you're not going until at least your chest feels better.'

'That could be ages. Look, those pills they gave me–'

'I've already talked to Patrick.'

'You did what?'

'I told him what happened and said you'll need a week off, at least.'

'How could you do that?'

'Really?' He paused as an elderly couple ambled by. 'I can do that because I don't want you to have to worry about work when you've just been in a fucking car accident. You're my wife.'

'You don't understand. Until I know what Victoria is after, I should–'

'Just stop it!' Mark growled. 'And keep going. We're standing in the middle of the car park arguing like idiots.'

I hobbled along behind him, my face hot with anger. Was he right? Did I need to just stop and let others look after me?

Mum was at home stocking our freezer with Tupperware containers. She'd made casseroles, pasta sauce and vegetable soup. Mark disappeared into his shed while Mum arranged me on the couch, propping up my leg on a pile of pillows.

'He's angry at me,' I murmured.

'Hmm?' Mum fluffed an extra pillow and tucked it under my head.

'Mark. I want to go to work but he won't let me.'

Mum laughed. 'Geez you're like your father.' She sat on the end of the couch and fixed me with a hard stare. 'Who cares about your job, Emily? Seriously, who cares? You could have been killed in that accident.' A lone tear dribbled down her cheek and she swiped it away. 'My darling girl. You've got a broken leg and a few bruises, and if I was ever going to be the praying hallelujah type, it would be now. You hear me?'

I smiled. 'Yes, I hear you.' It was on the tip of my tongue to tell her about Victoria, that I'd seen her peering through the car window, but I kept my mouth closed. I didn't want to upset her, or anyone. And I didn't want to be told again that I'd had a shock and probably imagined it. If I was imagining it, then no harm done.

But I was going to spend this week at home finding out all I could about this woman.

Chapter 13

Scrolling through Netflix with a sigh, I grimaced down at my plastered leg. The cast was surgical white where it sat propped against the fresh pillowcase, decorated with just one small rickety heart Mark had drawn with red pen. My knee, above the cast, was swollen and bruised.

Beside me, Bec slunk into the room grasping a bunch of flowers.

'I couldn't talk to you properly at the hospital, so...'

Waving her into the room, I turned back to the TV. 'Heard about any new shows?'

She took the remote from my fingers. 'You know I'm not big on TV.'

'I guess since I'm not a parent I have a lot more time than you–'

'Please,' Bec interrupted. 'I'm trying to apologise.' She toyed with the flowers, white daisies I recognised from her garden. She plucked the petal off a flower. 'You trusted me and I said the *one* thing I shouldn't have said to you. And I hate myself because now you've got yourself in an accident and it's all my fault.' Tossing the bouquet on the coffee table she burst into tears. 'I'm so sorry.' She knelt on the carpet in front of the couch and wiped her eyes.

I struggled up into a straighter position, jostling my leg against its pillow. 'It's not your fault at all. You don't know what happened when I got home.'

Bec raised her tear-streaked face. 'What happened?'

So I told her about Mark in the shed and the ensuing conversation. By the end, we were both sniffling, and Bec had a look of utter despair on her face. 'No wonder you took the day off.'

'I just should have told Mark where I was going, I guess,' I said ruefully. 'And now our car's totalled, my leg is broken and I don't know if I have a job. Not to mention my husband doesn't want a baby anymore.' I laughed harshly. 'Fucking great day.'

Bec squeezed in next to me on the couch. 'Don't worry about Mark, he's just tired of the whole thing, and it makes sense.' When I didn't respond, she rushed on. 'I know I don't really get it, because Poppy came along easily, but I can *imagine* what it must be like to–'

'It's fine, I know what you're saying. But what if this is it? I had the laparoscopy surgery and there's nothing wrong, so we just keep trying endlessly or else we start fertility treatment. I thought he was on board, he was building a cot and everything…'

Bec didn't say anything, just grabbed my hand and squeezed it in hers.

'I hear all these stories about it happening by *accident* and it makes me furious.'

Bec squeezed my hand harder.

'I don't want to break up over this, Bec. Mark and I need to be on the same page or we're not gonna make it.' I sighed. 'Anyway, I don't want to keep talking about it, despite making Mark feel like I'm obsessed.' I forced a laugh and released my hand from my sister's grip. 'I'm serious when I asked you about new TV shows before – what the hell can I do with this thing?' I indicated my cast and Bec shrugged.

'You can still limp around with the vacuum cleaner, use it as a crutch.'

We smiled at each other, and the remaining tension dissolved.

'How's the park fire?' I asked, and her smile dropped.

'It's out of control. It's so dry in there, it's just gone wild.'

'So if it spreads, does that mean you and Travis are in the firing line, or Mum and Dad?'

She faltered. 'Well, I don't know. Like you said, it's unpredictable.'

I pressed her. 'Are you worried?'

'No,' she shook her head. 'No, not yet.'

'And you and Dad?'

She grimaced. 'We're fine. It's all good. But Trav and I know more about fires than he does.'

'You think he doesn't listen to you? He does, you know.'

Her eyes softened. 'I know he does. We just clash sometimes, I guess.'

After Bec left, I practiced with the crutches around the house, eventually deciding to abandon them altogether once I was in the close confines of the kitchen. I set about making dinner, the simple task of reheating Mum's chicken casserole. When Mark came in and caught me, I rolled my eyes and let him take over, heading back to my spot on the couch that I was already sick of sitting in. I contemplated calling Patrick to talk to him myself about coming back to work, but figured it could wait until tomorrow after I'd hopefully had a proper night's sleep. Maybe I could even talk to Victoria, although it would be difficult to do so without asking her directly about the accident. *Was* it her? Now that I'd spent time in the hospital on strong painkillers, my memory was failing me. It seemed like a dream, and a crazy one at that. It just seemed impossible that anyone would do such a thing. I'd wanted to ask Bec, and at the same time, forget all about it. Torn between these two desires, how would I ever know the truth unless I confronted her?

Through the night I shifted constantly, my tender body protesting every movement as I tried to accommodate my cast and also get comfortable. I couldn't stop thinking about Victoria, and in the dead of night my suspicions didn't seem so ridiculous after all.

After Mark left for work in the morning, I fired up my laptop and logged into Facebook. He'd set me up for the day, placing items within reach as though I was an invalid with no access to crutches. While I appreciated his help, I was determined to get around just fine on my own. And the first thing I was going to do was try to find out more about Victoria.

In the search bar on Facebook I typed 'Victoria Shafer' and waited for the list of profiles to load. Scrolling, I peered closely at the profile pictures, opening new tabs for those that could possibly be her.

My eyes began to glaze over but I kept scrolling until I saw her.

Tori Shafer. The profile picture showed her blonde hair, cascading over one bare shoulder. Her eyes – *no mistaking those eyes* – were staring straight at the camera, in a daring, seductive way. Her mouth was open, teeth gleaming, as though she were sharing a sexy joke with the photographer.

I opened her profile and scanned the page, my heart pounding.

Scrolling, I searched for photos, personal details, posts… but there was nothing. Her page was private; the only available pictures were previous profile pictures, and they didn't shed much light. The same photo from my desk – the young girl with the ice cream. And another similar glamour shot – lips pursed, spaghetti straps over bronzed shoulders.

I contemplated sending her a friend request, but if my suspicions were right, she wouldn't accept it anyway.

I pushed away my computer with a frustrated grumble.

Grabbing my crutches, I took myself into the bathroom. I lifted my top and examined the bruises on my chest, the slash mark from the seat belt as the car hit. It was her face peering through the car window, wasn't it? Did she really do this to me? What I knew for sure was that she didn't like me – she cornered me in the gallery kitchen, and what I felt in those moments was *threatened.* I'd caught her checking out Mark online. So did she want my job or my husband? And she was clearly sleeping with Patrick, so what did that mean? It was a big leap from those things to running someone off the road. But it *was* her, wasn't it?

And she seemed to know about my medical appointments, and the snake. Did she let a brown snake loose in our house?

Had she been following me around? Had she been following Bec and Poppy around? I met my eyes in the mirror and shook my head. No one would do all these things. Clearly I was being ridiculous.

'I'm so glad you're home, I was bored today.' Leaning the crutches against the kitchen bench, I tossed the green salad I'd made and splashed over some vinaigrette dressing.

Mark dropped his wallet and keys in the bowl by the front door. I watched him head towards me, eyes downcast and lips pressed in a thin smile.

'You okay?' I asked. 'Crappy day?'

He pressed his face into my hair and inhaled. 'Yeah. I'm a bit tired that's all.'

We carried everything to the table, Mark helping me sit. I dished up our plates while Mark swigged his beer, staring out the window. 'Honey, what's wrong?'

I took a bite of salad and waited for him to answer.

'Work is a bit light on,' he eventually said, picking up his fork. 'I had some time today to think about stuff, and study this fire…'

'And?'

He took another swig of beer. 'Tomorrow's supposed to be forty degrees with a strong westerly.'

I swallowed a mouthful. 'So it could move east towards Bec's place.'

'Right. I don't have much work tomorrow so I might check in with Trav, see if I can help.'

'I don't want you going out to the fire front. You're not trained for that.'

'Yeah, I wouldn't do that. But I need to keep busy tomorrow, I need to help.'

Pushing away my plate, I frowned across the table. 'You're really worried about this fire? I didn't know it was that bad.'

Mark stood up and collected our plates. 'Tomorrow will tell.'

Mark sat up late, monitoring the weather and the emergency broadcast. When I woke, it was almost four and Mark was snoring in bed beside me. A glow permeated the bedroom; I fumbled for my crutches and swung myself out into the lounge room. The TV was still on and switched to the ABC. Across the bottom of the screen, bushfire warnings were listed in yellow, flashing names of towns not far away. Quietly I opened the front door and sure enough, the smell of smoke was strong, the char hitting the back of my throat. I was about to close the door when I noticed that across the street, Mrs Nichol's house lights were on. *Strange.* Who would be there at four am? I stepped out onto the concrete and squinting my eyes against the smoke, limped along the driveway, crutches pushing into my tender armpits. A shadow moved across Mrs Nichol's lounge room window and I flinched. *Who is that?* My foot teetered on the edge of the kerb. My heart skipped a beat. *What the hell am I doing?*

I rushed back inside, as quickly as my leg would allow, being careful not to slam the door behind me. Was I really about to go thumping on the door of my dead neighbour's house at four in the morning to see who was inside? Swearing under my breath, I flicked on the lights and moved into the kitchen. I sipped a glass of water at the sink, clearing my throat to get rid of the bushfire taste. It was then I noticed the black spots on my skin, on my singlet top and shorts. Ash. Ash falling from the sky from the nearby bushfire and here I am lured by my neighbour's lights. What was wrong with me?

'Em?'

I spun. I hadn't heard Mark enter the kitchen and he stood right behind me, face creased from the pillow and hair sticking up at all angles.

'Sorry if I woke you.'

'I thought I heard the front door.'

Shrugging, I tried to look nonchalant. 'I saw lights on at Mrs Nichol's house.'

He frowned and rubbed at his eyes. 'They're cleaning out her house. I saw Katrina there a couple of days ago.'

My face flushed with heat. It was the obvious answer, and yet I hadn't thought of it. My brain was stuck in this useless cycle of paranoia. But what had I expected? That Victoria was over there spying on me and formulating another devious plan?

'Right,' I managed to say, my voice croaky. I took another sip of water. 'It's smoky outside too, and look.' I showed him the spots of ash on my clothes. He rubbed at one with his fingers, leaving a charcoal smear.

'It's already hot. Want to put the air con on and come back to bed?' He reached for my glass and drained the remaining water from it. 'Or are you in pain or something?'

Shaking my head, I refilled the glass for him. 'No, I'm not in pain, but I'm going to stay up for a while.'

With a nod, he took the glass and padded out of the kitchen. I watched him go, wondering why things felt awkward with him at the moment. Was he angry at me for crashing the car? Upset about Mrs Nichol? Or was he worried about this fire?

The air conditioner kicked in, and with the cool air came a rush of clarity. I needed to talk to Victoria, I needed clear the air. So what if she'd been cyber-stalking my husband, that didn't make her a psychopath. If I talked to her properly then maybe I could let this paranoia go and relax while my leg healed. If I had to share my job with this woman then I had to make more of an effort. Trying to get pregnant *had* taken a toll, no matter how much I wanted to deny it. I couldn't blame Victoria for that.

#

The sun struggled to break through the smoke haze, giving the morning a heavy, sepia-toned quality that made me want to sit in front of the air conditioner in my underwear. Nevertheless, as soon as Mark left to see Travis, I pulled a loose skirt over my cast, tying up my hair and washing my face. Waiting for the taxi at the end of the driveway, I rehearsed what I could say to Victoria and then gave up. I shouldn't have to feel nervous around her. It was *my* job after all.

'Hello?'

Lifting my head, I saw Katrina waving from outside Mrs Nichol's house. She had pulled up by the kerb and opened the boot which was full of cardboard boxes. She crossed the street, nodding towards my crutches.

'What happened?'

'I had a car accident. But I'm okay. How are you going?'

She blew out a breath, lifting her fringe. 'Getting there. But I wanted to ask you something. Have you noticed anyone hanging around Mum's house?' She wrung her hands, cheeks glowing pink as though embarrassed. 'My husband thinks I'm being silly, that I'm grieving and imagining things, but I swear someone's been in the house.'

Swallowing, I remembered the lights on last night, the shadow moving across the window. 'Why do you say that?'

Katrina grimaced. 'Things feel off, I can't really explain it. I found a bottle of Coke in there yesterday, and I don't drink that. I'm the only one with a key, so I just don't see…'

'How would someone get in? Have you noticed any signs of a break in?'

She shook her head. 'But the door out the back can just be wrenched open really. I was on Mum's back about fixing that. The lock isn't secure, so I think someone could get in that way.' Planting her hands on her hips, she glanced across at her mother's house.

'I've noticed lights on at night, but I figured it was you. Mark thought it was you as well.'

Katrina swivelled to face me. 'Huh.' Brow furrowed, I could see the scenarios passing through her mind. 'Maybe Tony has a key. I'll have to check that. I knew I wasn't crazy.'

'What about how she…' I paused, swallowing past the lump in my throat. 'You said she was healthy.'

Katrina smiled sadly. 'The amount of medication I've found over there, and I had no idea. No idea. Seems like she wanted to protect us.'

I summoned an image of Mrs Nichol in the garden, pruning her roses in her big sun hat. She'd worked hard, right up until the end.

The taxi appeared, slowing to a stop. Katrina waved to the driver and reached over to pat me awkwardly on the shoulder. 'I hope your leg feels better.'

'Thanks,' I answered. 'And if you need anything, just ask.'

By the time I'd wrestled myself into my seat and deposited my crutches, Katrina was carrying a small stack of boxes up to her mother's door. I wiped the sweat off my face, trying to block what she'd said out of my mind. *Have you noticed anyone hanging around Mum's house? Things feel off, I can't really explain it.*

I couldn't think about that now, I had to concentrate on what I was going to say to Victoria.

The taxi pulled up in the gallery car park and the driver jumped out to help me with my crutches. A bearded man in his sixties, he wasn't familiar to me but knew who I was; he'd spent the drive explaining he'd attended high school with my dad.

'Say g'day to the old man, won't you, love?'

'Will do, Gary. Thanks for the help.' I levered myself up the gallery steps, through the small car park and towards the back door. My heart rate accelerated, and my hands slid on the handles of the crutches. I stopped for a minute to slow down my breathing and that's when I spotted it.

A Landcruiser.

The car from the accident.

Chapter 14

Rounding the white Landcruiser, I prodded a crutch at the black bull bar. No dents, but this was definitely the car. I'd seen it in the rear view mirror as it bore down on me, as it nudged my smaller car off the road.

Panic clawed at my throat. Dropping the crutches on the kerb, I hopped closer and shielded my eyes so I could look through the driver side window. The interior was clean; grey seat covers and nothing identifiable in the console.

'Emily?'

I looked up. Patrick and Victoria stood on the kerb. Patrick picked up my crutches and handed them to me. 'What are you doing?'

'Whose car is this?' I asked, snatching the crutches.

They exchanged a glance before Patrick spoke. 'Mine.'

Lifting my chin, I took a breath and prayed my voice didn't shake. 'And have you let Victoria borrow it by any chance?'

Victoria stood pale faced and silent. Patrick, on the other hand, looked amused. 'Why?'

'Because this is the car that did this to me,' I cried, frantically indicating my leg. 'This is the car that ran me off the road.'

He burst out laughing. 'You're kidding, right?'

'Does it look like I'm kidding?'

'You are saying that Victoria caused your car accident. In my car.' Patrick spoke slowly, as if he was speaking to a toddler.

I focused my attention on Victoria, who shifted her feet. 'Why did you do this to me? What could you possibly want from me? Is this about my job? Is this about Mark?'

Without saying anything, she glanced wide-eyed at Patrick, a picture of innocence. My blood boiled; my nostrils flared.

'Hey!' I shouted. 'I'm talking to you. I know it was you. I saw you through the window.'

'Emily.' Patrick held his hands out, palms forward, and stepped in front of me, blocking Victoria from view. 'That's enough.'

'I know it sounds crazy,' I pleaded with Patrick. 'But this is the car, I swear.'

'You've had a shock, I get it.' Patrick reached over to grab my arms but I recoiled from his touch. His expression changed from amused compassion to one of annoyance. 'Look, it's probably best that you go home and stay there until you're feeling better.'

'Don't talk to me like I'm an idiot,' I hissed.

'Ever since Victoria started you've treated her like crap. And now to come here and accuse her of doing this to steal your job?' Patrick shook his head. 'You need to leave. Now.'

Laughing harshly, I jabbed a finger into his chest. 'You

finally found someone who'll fuck you, so now you can't see anything else. But I've worked here for years, and you trusted me just fine until she came along.'

'You can't talk to me like that.' His voice shook, and instantly a hot flush of guilt crept into my cheeks. 'We might be the same age, Emily, but I'm still your boss, and you can't talk to me like that.'

Embarrassed, I looked away. 'I'm sorry.'

'We're going inside now. And you're leaving and not coming back. You hear me?' Patrick didn't wait for an answer, just spun on the heel of his shiny shoes and marched up the footpath. Victoria scurried after him, tossing me a concerned look as she disappeared inside the building.

I caught a taxi to Mum and Dad's, not relishing the thought of going home to an empty house to stew over what I'd said and done. I couldn't even remember exactly what I'd said, I'd been so angry and out of control when I saw the car that I'd just lost it.

The taxi driver was blessedly silent – someone I didn't know – so I stared out the window until the car pulled up in the driveway. The front yard was full of piled up branches, tall heaps of scraggly leaves and flaking bark. Drops of water rained over me as I hobbled along, and looking up, I saw a sprinkler tied to bricks sitting on the roof. The house was getting a good soaking for the fire, I realised, and a fresh wave of guilt washed over me. Ambushing Victoria and Patrick like that when a bushfire was closing in? Classy.

Mum met me at the door in a flour-dusted apron. 'What the hell are you doing here?'

'Lovely greeting, Mum.'

'No,' she shook her head. 'I mean, did you drive here? You can't drive with a bloody broken leg.' She craned her head around the doorway to scan the driveway out front.

'I called a taxi.'

'Well that's just as silly. I would have picked you up if you'd told me.' She tutted and hooked an arm through mine, helping me over to the kitchen table.

'What on earth are you doing?' I asked. The benches were piled with food; Tupperware containers and baggies and covered bowls. The kitchen was stifling, the oven on. 'Why are you baking in this heat?'

She flopped down on a chair across from me. 'Oh, it's stupid really, but we could have a tough few days ahead. I'm just trying to stock up a bit. I've made some salads and bread for the neighbours to make things a bit easier, although I guess that won't matter much if their house burns down.'

'You don't really think that will happen, do you?'

She smiled. 'No, but your sister has a way of rattling my cage.'

I smiled back. 'That's nice of you though, cooking for everyone.'

She flapped a hand. 'Have you had breakfast?'

'Yes. Thank you.'

'Did you really? What did you have?'

'Cereal,' I lied.

Frowning, she considered me from across the table. 'Then what's wrong?'

Opening my mouth, I sorted through what I should say. 'Things aren't great at the moment, with the accident and everything. I wanted to get out of the house.'

'You should be resting at home, you know.'

'I know.'

'Are you and Mark okay?'

'I don't know, Mum. But I'm pretty sure I've gotten myself fired.'

Mum leapt up from the table. 'That bloody bastard! He can't do that just because you need time off work, I'll wring his scrawny little–'

'Ma!' I interrupted. 'No, it's my fault. I had a crack at the new employee. But it doesn't matter anymore. Like everyone's been saying, it's just a job and it's not worth it.'

Hands on hips, Mum's lips were pressed into a thin line. 'I'll make us some coffee and we'll have a proper talk, all right?'

'Okay. Where's Dad?'

She stalked over to the kettle. 'He's with Travis, testing water pumps.'

'Oh, then Mark's there too, I think.'

I limped into the lounge room and stood gazing out the window. On the horizon, smoke blurred the trees that lined the hills, and the sky had an eerie pink glow. Against the wall, two suitcases sat bulging with belongings. 'Mum, will you leave or stay?' I called out, over the sound of boiling water and the clatter of porcelain.

'I'm leaving if it gets bad, and I'll be dragging your father along with me.'

I grinned, flopping down in an armchair. I held a cushion against my aching chest. Mum carried in a tray and set it on the coffee table, passing me a mug and a plate of biscuits. Curling up, I took a gulp of the hot liquid. Mum did the same in the armchair opposite, and for a few minutes we sat in silence, sipping and dunking. I looked across at her, at the beginnings of arthritis in her knuckles, the wrinkles around her mouth from her earlier smoking years, the hair greying at her temples – and I decided then to tell her.

'Mark and I have been trying for a baby for a long time, and it's not working.' Relief flooded my body, my shoulders loosening. My breastbone throbbed as I took a deep, cleansing breath, and I pressed the cushion tighter against it.

'Oh, darling.' Mum put down her mug and leaned forward in her armchair to grasp my hand. 'I'm sorry, love.'

'He wants to stop trying, to have a break. And part of me wants to as well, because I don't know how much longer I can do this. Every month it breaks my heart a little, to get that negative result again. Failing again.'

'You feel like a failure?'

Nodding, I continued, the words spilling out of me now. 'We've been to a doctor and everything, and there's no reason why it's not happening. It just *isn't*. And now it probably never will.' At that, my eyes filled with tears, and Mum pulled me gently into a hug. I rested my head on her chest and bawled, the way I did so many times growing up when I needed her comfort, and she held me without comment, without shushing me, just letting me cry it out.

Mum drove me home after feeding me an early lunch of potato salad and ham sandwiches. During the short drive into town, I sat and stared at the hazy landscape, eyes stinging from smoke and tears. We passed property after property of people preparing for fire – packing cars, setting up water pumps, up on roofs and cleaning gutters. I felt humbled by the sight, and exhausted. How much time I'd wasted worrying over things that concerned only myself, when I should have been making room for everyone else in my world. Every summer, the inhabitants of Alberton and all the surrounding towns prepared for bushfire, and it bonded them to the land and as a community. I felt a fierce surge of loyalty. Nothing else mattered except protecting family.

'Oh look, Mark's home,' Mum said as she pulled up in my driveway. 'Doesn't he have any work on?'

'Not today,' I murmured, my heart rate accelerating. 'He was with Travis, remember?' But why was he home already? Did he know what I'd done?

Mum carried my handbag and a tub of pasta salad while I struggled along with my crutches. Inside, Mark glowered over a beer at the kitchen table. Mum kissed us both and left quickly and quietly, obviously not wanting to interfere. As soon as the front door clicked shut behind her, Mark stood up and faced me.

'Patrick called me.'

My stomach dropped. 'Oh.'

'What the hell were you thinking?' His face was thunderous; I'd never seen him so angry. 'Your good-natured teasing is one thing, but the shit you said to him… and to her for that matter…'

'I know,' I whispered, my face hot. 'I'm sorry, I shouldn't have gone there. I was trying to do the right thing, but it backfired. I saw the car there, in the car park, and I *knew* it was her that caused the accident. I suspected it was, and then the car was there. And he said it was his, and it all made sense—'

'It doesn't make sense,' Mark snapped. 'It doesn't make sense at all. You can't piss off Patrick, you know that. His family owns everything, including where we live.' He slapped the wall for emphasis. 'You've lost your job, you know that.'

'I'll get it back–' I began.

'No, you won't,' Mark interrupted. 'You lost your job as soon as he brought Victoria in and we both know it. Every time I see her she's perfectly nice, but you've just had it in for her from day one–'

'What do you mean *every time* you see her?' I interrupted, my mind racing, mentally counting back the encounters I knew about.

'See!' Mark cried. 'That's what I'm talking about. I've seen her a few times, at work, at the supermarket, normal stuff.' He swore, and my hot face grew warmer. 'You can't be in the same place as her, it'll never work.'

A flush of anger overtook my shame, and I narrowed my eyes. 'Okay, *master*, what do you propose then?'

'That you kiss Patrick's arse to get a good reference and then steer clear of Victoria from now on. And not to mention that you take care of your damn leg!'

'Right, thanks for that,' I spat. 'How about taking my side?'

'Really?' he shouted. 'I'm always on your side, but you're making it hard at the moment!'

'You don't believe me!' I shouted back. 'That woman hates me and she ran me off the road in Patrick's car. I don't know why, but I know it was her. I haven't even told you everything and you still don't believe me!'

'What are you talking about?'

'How she was looking at pictures of you online, and how

Katrina said someone's breaking into Mrs Nichol's house–'

'So that's Victoria too? She's spying on you from across the street too?'

'I don't know, but no matter what I say to you, you make me feel like a fucking idiot!'

'Good thing you won't be seeing her anymore then.'

We fell into a tense silence, facing each other across the table and the huge tub of Mum's pasta salad in the middle.

'So this is how it's going to go?' I asked eventually. 'You tell me what to do and I have to toe the line?'

Mark scoffed. 'You can't be serious. You crossed the line today with Patrick and that has nothing to do with me.'

'But you're here. You came back to tell me off?'

Mark swallowed. 'No, I'm here because I don't have a job. There's not enough work for me at the moment.'

'What?' I stuttered. 'You said that today you were seeing Travis because you're worried about the fire.'

'Yeah, I did. And while I was out the boss called me with an update, and there's no work for me.'

'Just you? What about the others? I mean, if I can't work at the moment as well, then we can't afford–'

'Because nobody cares,' he interrupted. 'I told my boss about your leg, that you can't work, but he doesn't care. Damo has another kid on the way, Smithy's wife is sick… everyone has something.' With a sigh, Mark sat, reaching for his beer and taking a long swig.

I sat across from him, resting my arms across the Tupperware lid, feeling the cool chill of the plastic under my hot palms. 'When will you get more work?'

'Things are quiet, like every January. Jobs are being finished off or they haven't started yet. No one wants to be building a house over the summer holidays. So it could be a few weeks, I don't know. Could be longer.'

'You don't know what's coming up?'

'There's not enough coming up, is what I'm saying.'

'So what are we going to do?'

Mark looked up, and his face was softer, his eyes wide and imploring. 'Please, *please*, stay away from Victoria. We don't need that problem right now.'

'I promise. But do we need to look for somewhere cheaper to live? Can you ask around, pick up some extra work on the side? Travis would know heaps of tradies, there might be some casual work around.'

Mark pushed his empty bottle away. 'Everyone's struggling at the moment, hon. But I'll try. I'll make some calls.'

Chapter 15

That afternoon I packed up our irreplaceable belongings. Our paperwork and photos, sentimental gifts and essential stuff like a change of clothes and toiletries. If we had to flee the fire, which was unlikely living in town, we'd be ready. And if we had to move house, well then, I'd made a head start. I juggled the box and suitcase into the spare room, shutting the door behind me.

At dusk, I grabbed two forks and met Mark on the back step. We sat and ate from the container of pasta salad, watching the sprinkler soak the grass. The smoke had eased but still cloaked the perimeter of the yard, the tree trunks appearing slightly blurred. I'd become used to the tickle in my throat throughout the day – where it invaded even the closed-up house – and it was a reminder of what was happening out there, to those residents not too far away from us.

Mark and I didn't speak, each caught up in our own thoughts and worries. Despite my promise to Mark, and despite trying to forget, I couldn't get the look on Victoria's face out of my mind. She had looked upset and frightened, perhaps frightened of me. She wasn't indignant or she didn't look guilty. Was I wrong about her? And Patrick – I insulted him for taking a partner where he could find one. I felt dirty inside, cheap for using that as a reason to attack him.

As the already hazy sun disappeared, and I grabbed the handrail to take myself inside, Mark took his big rectangular pencil from his shirt pocket and marked my cast with another small love heart. We shared a smile in the twilight; I knew everything would be okay between us.

I hobbled through the darkened house – curtains shut against the heat – and made for the couch to prop up my leg. I hadn't taken any painkillers since the morning, and my body was protesting, the heavy throb vibrating through my whole body. Easing my phone out of my skirt pocket, I tried to call Bec. I'd been trying all afternoon with no success. This time, she answered.

'Hey, update me. What's happening?'

'Yeah, I've been meaning to call you, Em, sorry. My God, we've been arguing about what to do, but we've prepared the house as much as we can so we're going to go in. Everything's set up at Alberton Oval, so we'll hitch a ride out to the fire from there.'

'And Poppy?'

'Can you have her?'

'Of course. Bring her over. When are you going?'

'Tonight, so if we can bring her over soon then we can go to the oval from your place.'

'Okay. What about Mum and Dad? Have you talked to them?'

'No, would you mind? We thought of taking Poppy to

their place, because of your leg, but we'd prefer knowing she was safe in the centre of town.'

'Mark's here to help me so it's fine. I'll call them, make sure they're okay.'

'Thanks. We're packing up some stuff. Be there soon.'

Bec hung up in my ear and I immediately called Mum. Her phone rang into voicemail so I tried Dad.

'You all right, love?'

'We're fine, Dad. Just checking on the both of you. And I wanted to let you know we're having Poppy tonight; Bec and Travis are going out to the fire.'

'Righto. Your mum is glued to the radio right now. We should be right here though, I reckon.'

'Please come here if you're not sure. Don't hesitate, Dad, it's not worth it.'

Dad was quiet a minute, then agreed. 'You look after our little girl, won't you?'

We said our goodbyes and I hung up with a lump of unease in my throat. We'd been through this before, but the fire had never been as close, or as large.

On TV, the ABC was reporting on a political scandal but at the bottom of the screen, bushfire updates were highlighted in yellow and scrolling endlessly. Besides our fire, there were six others burning in our area of the state, two of them new fires that had started from flying embers from the park fire. And there it was, scrolling along with a list of other nearby townships told to be on alert: Alberton.

'Mark!'

He appeared beside me, focusing on the screen, and immediately stilled. 'That's not good.'

'Bec and Trav are bringing Poppy.'

'They're going out to the fire?'

'Yeah.'

'Your folks?'

'They're okay. They're staying put.'

'They should be right. These spot fires aren't that close to them.'

I looked at him. 'I have a bad feeling about this one.'

Bec and Travis arrived quickly and quietly, Travis cradling a sleeping Poppy in his arms. Mark led Travis into our bedroom to tuck her into bed. Bec put down a *Frozen* backpack, along with a bigger bag.

'You should have everything you need. Change of clothes, some snacks, and there's some extra pull-ups so she won't wet your bed.' She flicked a hand in the direction of my bedroom. 'She's wearing some now, by the way. I'm leaving you my car, so if there's an emergency or whatever, you'll have a car if Mark isn't here.' She placed the keys next to the bags.

'All good, thanks. Don't worry about us.'

Bec nodded, but she looked distracted, her eyes darting around the lounge room. She got this way sometimes during fire season, but usually she approached the threat with calmness.

'You okay?' I asked.

Bec blew out her cheeks. 'Not really. I have to tell you something.' The bedroom door creaked shut and in the distance, I heard Mark and Travis talking softly. Bec stepped closer, speaking rapidly. 'I've put off telling you, but I have to tell you now and I need you to be okay with it.'

I nodded, grabbing her hand to keep her talking.

'Travis and I really want a sibling for Poppy, so we're

trying again. I didn't want to tell you, but I *have* to tell you. I can't keep a secret from you. And I'm sorry, and I wish I could make things better for you–'

The boys stepped gingerly into the lounge room, glancing awkwardly between us.

'It's okay,' I whispered to Bec, even though I wasn't sure how to feel. Mostly I just wanted to calm her down, to send her off with the assurance that everything was all right.

'Are you sure? I don't want this to come between us.'

I nodded briefly, and Bec's face relaxed, her shoulders drooping a little. She stepped closer, murmuring into my ear, 'but that's something you can still do with that cast on, you know, just lie on your back.'

I forced a smile, appreciating the attempt to lighten the mood, despite the fact that Mark hadn't touched me in that way since that night he got stoned in the shed. I'd told Bec what he said about having a break from trying, but hope still shone in her eyes that everything would work out for all of us.

'We should go,' Travis said finally, and the moment was over, and as Mark and I watched Travis's ute back down the driveway, headlights blurring through the smoke, Mark wrapped an arm around my shoulders and pulled me to him.

'Anything we need to talk about?' he asked, waving in response to the quick jab of the car horn.

'No, all good. Let's get out of this smoke.'

Inside, I propped up my leg in front of the news, laptop perched on the other one. Mark did the same, and we were united this night, sitting up late, staying up to date to protect our niece.

The lights were on again at Mrs Nichol's house. I stood at the window, remembering what Katrina had said. Was it her this time, sorting out her mother's things? Or was someone else really over there?

I cleared my throat against the ever-present tickle of smoke. I checked over my shoulder; Mark and Poppy were fast asleep, arms and legs akimbo, sheet thrown off the mattress. Smiling, I hobbled down the hall to the bathroom and peered into the mirror at my sweat-shiny face. It was difficult to wash myself properly with the cast, and I'd been getting Mark to help me in and out of the bath. Tonight, despite desperately needing a shower, I settled for a cold washcloth, wiping my face, armpits and between my legs. Shaking out my lank and greasy hair from its ponytail, I made a mental note to wash it in the morning.

Changing into a tank top and boxer shorts, I crawled gingerly into bed, turning on my right side to protect my leg. Poppy's small body radiated heat from where she lay sprawled between us; I wrapped the cool pillow around my head and blew out a breath. The fan in the corner wasn't doing much, and the smell of smoke was hard to ignore.

I fell into a fitful sleep, and found myself walking – leg unbroken – through a dark house. It smelt of dust, of sweat and fear, but I crept forward anyway, navigating my way around shadowy objects lurking in the darkness. A dark-panelled china cabinet, an old lumpy recliner, a glass-topped coffee table. I felt a breeze and moved eagerly towards it. The window was open, wind blowing the curtain out into the room. And behind the curtain, a shape, moving silently and smoothly along the window sill. Back and forth it went, and I froze, watching it, trying to figure out what it was. When it stopped moving, I held my breath, waiting and knowing that something was about to happen. Two bright green spots, like lasers, beamed out from the window sill. *Eyes*. And it was then I realised what it was, *who* it was. The cat cocked its head, testing me, waiting for me to make a move. But I dared not move. I still didn't know what she wanted, and why she was watching me.

'Emily,' the cat breathed, and sprung out from behind the curtain. It was then that I ran, sprinting for the front door and finding it locked. I pummelled it with my fists, but I could feel her behind me, lighting me up with her green eyes.

Chapter 16

'Emily.'

I woke with a weight on my tender chest and gasped for a breath, almost hitting out at the object before remembering.

Poppy.

When I opened my eyes, I met hers, her face only inches away from mine. She giggled, using a hand to softly pat my face. Up close, I could see the delicate blue veins in her eyelids, the velvety down on her skin glowing golden in the morning light.

'Look who's awake,' I croaked, gently moving her away from my bruises.

'Uncle Mark says I can have Froot Loops.'

'Lucky duck,' I smiled, and she leapt from the bed and ran from the bedroom with an ecstatic shriek.

I stayed still for a minute listening to the sounds from the kitchen; Mark's laugh, the rattle of bowls and clinking of cutlery. I could hear the news too – the unmistakable drone of a newsreader's voice. I struggled out of bed and went to the window. Outside, white. Smoke moved like fog through the front garden, so thick I could barely see the road or the houses across the street. Mrs Nichol's house, the site of my nightmare, was a mere shadow, just a hint of a structure in the distance. Somehow this was scarier than if I'd been able to see it clearly, as if I was stuck in some kind of foggy, gothic scene.

Grabbing my crutches from where they leant against the wall, I made my slow journey out into the kitchen, my armpits burning from the pressure of the pads. I kissed Poppy, inhaling the warmth from her soft hair. Mark passed me a coffee and we exchanged a smile. At the table, the three of us sat as a family and I enjoyed the illusion, sipping from my mug and watching Poppy experimentally swirl a finger through her bowl of Froot Loops. Across the room, however, the TV flashed fire warnings across the screen – a kick of reality that shot through my veins faster than the caffeine.

'Any news?' I asked Mark, keeping an eye on Poppy. She plucked an orange loop from the lake of milk and crunched into it, oblivious to the adult talk at the table.

'Not really,' he answered. 'I feel like I should be doing something, seeing if I can help anyone. But I don't want to leave you alone.' He glanced at his niece and sighed.

'Hey, you don't have to worry about that part. But where would you go?'

'I could start by checking on your folks.'

I shrugged, draining my coffee. 'It's up to you and the weather, I guess, and how that changes. What have you heard?'

He checked on Poppy again before pushing his mug

away. 'It's supposed to reach thirty-eight today with strong gusty winds.'

'Damn.' I thought of Bec and Travis's house, unmanned out of town. If their house came under ember attack and they chose to stay with the fire front, they could lose the lot.

Mark spent the next while on the phone; I sat on the couch and helped dress Poppy in a fresh pink skirt and glittery t-shirt. I encouraged her to sit beside me on the couch afterwards and play with her dolls. She seemed to understand that I couldn't run around and parked herself next to me, twirling her Elsa doll and jabbering away. I'd switched on some cartoons – knowing that Mark was monitoring the fire with his phone – and she alternated her attention between the TV and her toys.

Mark left at lunch time, scarfing down a salad sandwich and dumping his plate in the sink while Poppy and I were still eating ours.

'I'll check on the farmhouse, and then I'll see your parents. There's a meeting at the fire station your dad is going to, and I'll probably go with him.' He gathered up his keys, wallet, sunglasses. 'Are you sure you'll be okay here on your own?'

I nodded. 'We're safe here, and we'll just take it easy, won't we, Pops?'

'We can watch *Frozen*,' she cried, and a piece of cucumber flew out of her mouth and slapped on to the table.

'See?' I stifled a grin and Mark smiled back.

He came over and kissed us both. 'I don't know when I'll be back, but promise you'll call me if you need me to come home.'

'I will.' Watching him go, I realised I hadn't gotten his help to bathe yet. *Damn. At least I can wash my hair in the sink.*

I planted Poppy in front of ABC Kids while I washed my hair, hunched forward over the bathroom basin. Working as quickly as I could, I rinsed out the suds, grabbed a towel from the rack and rubbed at my head, then used it to wipe up the water around the sink. Poppy wrapped her arms around my cast, startling me, asking about *Frozen*. So with a plate of Oreos, we arranged ourselves back on the couch and started the movie.

#

Poppy woke me with an urgent whisper. 'There's a baby.'

'What?' Lifting my head from the back of the couch, I rubbed at my stiff neck. I hadn't even realised I'd fallen asleep, and certainly hadn't meant to, and a glance at the TV thankfully confirmed the movie was still in its early stages. I hadn't been out for long.

Poppy shook me again. 'Baby,' she insisted.

I sat up, looking around. 'Where?'

But then I heard it, the mewling of a newborn's cry.

I jumped to my feet, forgetting my leg for a moment, and bit back a curse at the jolt of pain. Poppy followed suit and we stood silently, listening. Poppy pointed to the backyard, and I cocked my head, staring at the door off the kitchen. She was right. That was where the crying was coming from.

'Stay here, honey.'

She jumped on the spot for a minute, clearly excited to

see the baby, but I shot her a stern look as I grabbed my crutches. With a dramatic huff, she flopped onto the lounge room floor.

I hobbled into the kitchen, listening to the plaintive cries that went on without pause. At the back door I lingered, and my stomach turned. Something felt off; there was no logical reason a baby could possibly be on our back doorstep.

'Poppy, stay there and I'll just be a minute,' I called. No answer. She had probably lost interest and was absorbed back in the movie. Or I couldn't hear her over the shrill cries.

Putting my hand on the knob, I edged the door open and peered through the crack. I waved a hand through the smoke but there was nothing there, no mysterious bassinet like when a baby was dumped in the movies. I stepped out and looked around, trying to figure out where the sound was coming from. Dropping my crutches, I used the handrail to lever myself down the steps and into the backyard. The grass was littered with burnt leaves, and ash that looked like black snow. But there was no baby.

I frowned. *What the hell?* Coughing against the bushfire smoke I searched the shrubbery on the side of the steps that hugged the side of the house. As I was about to give up, I spotted it. A small, black object caught the weak light. Plucking it from the garden bed, I stared at it. It was a mobile phone, and the screen showed it was playing a recording. A recording of a baby crying. I pressed stop and immediately the screaming ceased. My heart was thumping and a wave of terror rode through me. I didn't understand, but my legs propelled me back towards the house. Tossing the phone to the ground, I swung my leg ahead of me, grabbing my crutches and stumbling back into the kitchen. All I knew was I had to get back into the house, lock the door and call the police.

'Poppy?' I called. 'You okay, sweetheart?'

No answer. Elsa was singing, the movie playing on.

I locked the kitchen door and hobbled through the kitchen and into the lounge. The room was empty.

'Poppy?'

With a grunt, I made my way up the hallway, checking the toilet and the bathroom. Empty.

'Poppy? Answer me, honey!'

The bedroom. Empty.

The spare room. Empty.

Back in the lounge room, and still I couldn't see her anywhere.

'Don't hide from me, Pops. Please come here.'

Nothing.

The smell of smoke was strong, the haze hanging in a ghostly cloud near the ceiling. And then I saw it.

The front door was open.

Chapter 17

'Poppy!' I yelled. Why would she go out the front? She knew not to do that. As fast as I could, I let myself through the door and, swivelling my head, searched the driveway and the street. There was no sight of her, but with the road shrouded in smoke, I couldn't see very far into the distance. Sweat was breaking out on my upper lip, my throat tightening and threatening tears.

'Poppy!' I screamed. 'Poppy!' I screamed as hard as I could. What did I do now? I couldn't run after her. She never came out the front on her own, she wouldn't. But I knew in my bones that she hadn't. Someone had taken her.

The baby. The crying.

A distraction.

'Oh my god.' I froze on the spot, my body vibrating with adrenaline but not knowing what to do. Swearing, I hobbled back into the house and grabbed for my mobile phone, bag and Bec's car keys. I dialled Mark's number, but hung up before he answered.

Someone had taken my niece. And I knew who it was. It

had to be her. Didn't it? The things she'd said in the kitchen, the delivery of the baby seat, the car accident, the fucking snake? Could it all have been her? Why? I couldn't work it out. Nothing made sense. But if I could find Poppy without alarming Mark, or calling the police, then… then what?

Move, my head was screaming. *Move!*

I pressed a hand against my chest, trying to calm my heart. I dropped my crutches on the floor and hurried out of the house as quickly as I could on my painful leg. I jumped into Bec's car, grateful it was an automatic and it was my left leg in the cast; at least I could use my right foot on the pedals.

Switching on the headlights I crept along the street, hunching over the wheel to peer through the windscreen. The houses were eerily quiet, cloaked and ghostly, with no one outside doing their usual things; watering plants, mowing lawns, sweeping paths. I could see no people at all, and certainly no little girl.

Eyes burning, I pulled over, leaving the engine idling. *What do I do? Where do I go?* I squeezed the phone in my fist and with my other hand I rubbed at my stinging eyes. It wasn't good for anyone to be out in this smoke, and my heart hammered with the thought of Poppy's small lungs breathing this in.

I had to find her. I had to get her back.

Call the police!

No. I ignored my better judgement and gunned the engine, pulling back out into the street. This was my first time driving since the accident, but I didn't have time to be nervous or hesitant. I slammed through intersections, finally screeching to a stop in the gallery car park. The few minutes' drive to work had never felt so long, so excruciating. And although the roads were quiet, I wanted to scream at the few people who were out: 'Don't you know this is an emergency?'

My body felt tight enough to break, and my leg throbbed. The car park was empty, and I took a second to ponder over why Patrick wouldn't be at work. He lived on The Grove, perched high over the town, but their properties were clear of bush. They wanted the town to see them up there, lording it over the little people. The Grove would be safe from the fire.

Thankfully I still had my key to the gallery, and I unlocked the back door and stepped inside. It was dark and cool, but I didn't take any time to appreciate it, limping into the office. I was using the cast as a shoe now, and the vibration as it connected with the floor jolted my leg in agony. But there was no choice.

At my desk, or Victoria's desk, I dropped my weary body down into the chair and switched on the computer. I figured my only chance to find Poppy before I relented and called someone was to find out where Victoria lived. I hoped above everything that I'd find Poppy there, but at the same time, I wanted to be wrong. But if Victoria hadn't taken her, then who had? And was I making a huge mistake by not calling for help? Should I have called the police by now to report a missing child?

Fingers tapping madly on the keyboard, I looked up her staff record. There was no phone number, but there was an address. Scrabbling for a discarded envelope I scrawled her address on it, even though I knew exactly where it was. It wasn't far away. Patrick's family owned her townhouse, and the strip of them in her street. They were remarkably similar to mine and Mark's, and the realisation churned my stomach even more. She really had taken my place, and now she had taken my niece.

My phone rang, startling me. Glancing at the screen I saw it was Mark and answered. I had to tell him. If I was wrong, I would never forgive myself.

'Poppy's gone, Mark. I think Victoria's taken her.' I didn't wait for him to answer, ploughing on. 'I'm going to her place, I've got her address, but I could be wrong. I don't know. There was a recording of a baby crying—' I shook my head. 'I don't have time to explain everything now.'

'I'm calling the police,' I heard Mark say. 'Where are you?'

'At the gallery getting her address. I'm going there now.' I hung up, trying to ignore the doubt and outrage in his voice.

I drove to Green Street, and found the number on her mailbox. Lights glowed in the townhouse next door, but Victoria's looked quiet, blinds drawn over the windows. I parked at the kerb, even though the walk to the front door looked excruciatingly long. Perhaps I should have roared up the driveway in Bec's car; it wasn't as though I could stealthily creep up without being seen, not with the awkward cast on my leg.

The exterior of the townhouse was so similar to ours, with its dark brick and low-maintenance garden beds. This place wasn't as neat; paths unswept and scattered with bark and leaves, weeds sprouting around the shrubs. The garage door was pulled down so it was impossible to see if there was a car inside. There was no evidence that anyone was home, but I had to check.

Swinging the car door open, I wrenched the keys from the ignition and snatched up my phone. Suppressing an initial cough in the smoky air, I concentrated on my indignation and fear for Poppy. It was not the time for trepidation.

My leg was throbbing, my chest aching. I wrapped an arm across my ribs and held them tight as I hobbled up the driveway. I pounded on the front door with my fist, and behind me a small bird startled, fluttering its wings and taking off.

'Hello?' I called, my voice hoarse from the smoke. At the lounge room window I tried to peer through the crack in the blind, but the interior was dark. 'Hello?' I yelled. 'Poppy?'

Swearing, I made my way around the house, moving awkwardly but as quickly as I could. A side gate was open, standing eerily still. I moved through it, and onto a concrete patio that led to a sliding glass door. The glass was uncovered and I looked inside, cupping my hands around my face. I was struck then by the gesture – the same as on the day this woman ran me off the road and did the same thing through my car window. Rage bloomed.

'Open the door, you psycho!' I screamed, thumping a fist. I reached for the handle and shook it, and to my shock the door screeched open, rattling along its track. I gaped for just a moment, then stepped over the threshold.

What struck me first was the smell – a mixture of sweat and garbage that made me almost gag as I stared around the kitchen I'd walked into. It was a mirror image of ours, except here the bin was overflowing, the benches were stacked with dirty dishes, the sink filled with old sludgy brown washing-up water. A small movement on the stove caught my eye and I looked closer. A greasy saucepan crawled with maggots.

I coughed, covering my mouth to hold back vomit. *Please don't let Poppy be in this place.* I rushed into the lounge room, past an empty and stained couch, a coffee table cluttered with wine bottles and pizza boxes. In the hallway, I looked left and right, but I knew where to go. The floor plan was identical to ours. In her bedroom, her bed was unmade and strewn with clothes. Mugs and crumby plates were scattered around, and the room stunk of sweat, of an unwashed person. *Yet at work she was so immaculate.*

And on the bedside table, a framed photo. The same girl from Victoria's Facebook page, only this time, cradled in Victoria's lap. Painted hearts decorated the frame, a glittery angel in the corner, and the letters *R.I.P.*

I stood a moment, staring at it, and finally, the pieces of the puzzle started to slide into place. Stumbling from the room, I changed direction, checking a similarly filthy bathroom and toilet, taking shallow breaths to fight the stench.

At the end of the hallway, the door to the spare room stood closed. I paused, terrified of what I might find behind it, then turned the knob.

Inside, the room was softly lit by fairy lights. A bed with a pink canopy sat beside a shelf lined with teddies and dolls wearing tutus. Pink and red rugs covered the floor, and scattered around the room were fairies and ballerinas. On the wall, a huge castle had been painted.

The room was sparkling clean.

And it was identical to Poppy's bedroom.

Hunching forward, I grabbed at my stomach and tried not to scream.

I'd been right, *of course* I had. This woman was sick. She had stolen my niece. And why? To replace her daughter who died?

But they weren't here. So where were they?

Thinking quickly, I snapped some pictures with my phone and got the hell out of there, pulling the sliding door shut as I left. Back in Bec's car, I called Mark.

'Where are you? What's her address? Are you still there?' He fired the questions at me before I could say anything.

'I'm sending you some pictures from Victoria's house,' I answered, putting him on speaker while I texted him the photos.

'What the fuck…' I heard him breathe. 'That's inside her house?'

'Yes, and Poppy's not here. No one is here.'

'I'm at the police station, Em, you need to come here now.'

My heart leapt. 'Have you found her?'

'No, but the police are looking for her now, okay? Please come here and be with me. You shouldn't be driving.'

'I have to find her, Mark. Have you been to Bec's? That's the only other place I can think of, that maybe she took her there to get some clothes or toys?'

'I haven't been to the farmhouse yet, but hon, you can't go out that way, it's too dangerous. Bec and Trav are heading back to the house because the fire's getting closer.' He hesitated. 'And Victoria's obviously unstable, Em. Just come here, please.'

'I told you there was something wrong with this woman,' I snapped. 'But you didn't believe me. I'm going out to Bec's.'

'Then I'll meet you there.'

I tossed my phone onto the passenger seat.

Chapter 18

On the way out of town I had no choice but to drive slowly. The smoke was getting thicker and the sun was obscured, casting the landscape into deep shadow. The car quickly filled with smoke, and I coughed and wheezed through it, my lungs drying out, my eyes burning. But I couldn't drive any faster; I could barely see where I was going.

Headlights on, I crawled along the gravel road that led to my sister's. I was well aware that I was driving right into danger, and a logical person wouldn't do that. But Victoria wasn't logical, clearly. If she hadn't brought Poppy home, then I had run out of ideas. Hopefully by the time I got to Bec's, she and Travis would be there, and Poppy would be safe in their arms.

My stomach flipped as I rolled along the driveway. A car sat in front of the house, unfamiliar, its make obscured by the smoke. Wrenching the keys from the ignition I leapt out of the car, biting back a scream as my cast thumped the gravel. The blast of heat was like a furnace, almost knocking me off my feet. I could hear the fire here too, and it sounded close.

I pulled my t-shirt up over my nose and mouth and dragged myself up the steps to the front door.

I used the key to let myself in, fingers shaking in my panic, entering the dim hallway. It was hotter inside than out, and I took a breath, my eyes adjusting as I neared the family room. All the curtains were drawn but the house was so familiar; I dodged furniture as I checked for people, any movement. I wasn't certain who owned the car outside; it could have been borrowed to ferry Bec and Travis home, or Mark could have driven it from the police station – maybe it was an officer's car? I didn't know, but instinct told me not to call out, to check the house before I made a decision about what to do next.

I headed straight for Poppy's room and found it empty, with everything in place. I scanned the room for missing items, but she had so many toys I couldn't tell. My dry throat drew me to the kitchen where I grabbed a glass and filled it at the sink. Lifting the blind on the kitchen window, I peered out into the backyard and froze. On the horizon beyond the paddocks, a wall of flames. It was difficult to determine the distance, but I had never been this close to a fire, and after living in the country my whole life, I knew how fast they could move.

Dropping the glass in the sink, I hobbled as fast as I could to the back door, flinging it open. The angry roar was louder back here, and my stomach flipped with fear. Stepping out onto the back veranda, I scanned the backyard for signs of life.

And I found it.

A dark shape hunched under the slide and swing set. Blurred in the smoke, I couldn't tell who it was, but it was human. A scorching gust of wind buffeted the house, and me, baking me in its intense heat. I ran, gritting my teeth against the agony in my leg. As I got closer, the shape took on definition. Victoria kneeled over Poppy, who wasn't moving.

'Get off her!' I screamed. I dove towards Victoria, tackling her at the waist and driving her back from where Poppy lay on the ground.

Over the ominous groan of the wind, I could hear sirens nearby. *Please.*

'She's not moving!' Victoria squealed, struggling out of my grip. 'My baby's not moving!' Eyes wild, she looked towards me but through me. 'It's happening again. No, no, no, no, no…'

'Move away,' I yelled, my voice cracking. 'Let me help her.'

Victoria looked up. Dressed all in black, blond hair scraped into a tight bun, her pale face glowed like the moon in the dark afternoon. She looked broken, devastated, and far away.

A bolt of fear shot through me, and shoving Victoria away, I ran the last few steps to Poppy's prone body. She was unconscious, but her small chest was moving. She was alive.

'Victoria, listen to me.'

'She's my Lily.'

'No, she's Poppy, and she doesn't belong to you. You are hurting her and you don't want to do that.'

'I am not hurting her,' Victoria snarled, teeth flashing. 'I'm helping her, I'm–'

'We need to get her inside, do you hear me?' I shouted

over the roar. 'The fire's coming.'

Victoria looked up, head swivelling, eyes widening when she noticed the flames on the horizon. 'I was trying to do the right thing. I didn't know–'

'I'm going to carry her inside now.' Leaning forward I grabbed my niece, bundling her body into my arms. She still wore the clothes I'd dressed her in this morning, and my mind raced as I wondered what she had endured since being in Victoria's company. What had the woman done to her?

The sirens shrieked, and through the back windows of the house, red and blue lights flashed as two cars pulled in. Turning my back on Victoria, I clutched Poppy and hobbled as quickly as I could towards the back veranda, my leg weakening and beginning to give way, my eyes burning and blurring with tears.

'Em!' Mark screamed, his boots thumping on the floorboards. I saw him a moment later, as he barrelled into the lounge room and swooped on Poppy, lowering her to the floor. 'In here,' he cried. I dropped to the floor beside him, pain overwhelming me now that I knew Poppy was safe.

Uniformed people rushed in, paramedics and police officers, crowding around us. Someone rushed out into the backyard. I fought against the urge to vomit, focusing on the sounds around me and trying to keep my leg still.

Beside me, Mark was nudged aside so paramedics could attend to Poppy. Then I heard her cough, and draw in a ragged breath.

My heart swelled, my body relaxed.

Mark grabbed my hand. 'She's okay, Em,' he gasped, looming over me. 'I'm so sorry I didn't listen to you.'

Lifting my head, I watched over his shoulder as a police

officer ran full pelt through the backyard. He was chasing Victoria into the paddocks, where she ran towards the fire.

She glanced over her shoulder as she stumbled forward, mouth wide open in a scream I couldn't hear over the roar of the flames. The officer was gaining on her, but Victoria was gathering speed.

I watched, until Victoria's dark clothing was completely obscured by the smoke and she wasn't visible anymore.

#

They found Victoria's body the next morning, after the CFA had successfully fought back the flames. Bec's house was saved, but others in town weren't as lucky. Poppy had suffered smoke inhalation and a bump to the head as she tried to run away from Victoria. But for the most part she was unhurt, and the doctor assured everyone she would make a full recovery.

Alberton, the town I had grown up in and knew so well, all pulled together in the face of tragedy. Even Patrick's family softened and opened their wallets and helped house the families who had lost their homes.

Patrick visited me in the hospital once he'd heard about Victoria. I was cuddled up with Bec and Poppy when he slunk through the door and grovelled with apologies that he hadn't listened to me when I tried to tell him about Victoria. I had an apology for him too, and we parted with a truce – we didn't really like each other, but we were used to each other, and I would be a part of the gallery as long as I wanted to be. I didn't know how long that would be, but I needed to work for our marriage right now, support us until Mark was settled back at work and we had figured out what to do about a baby.

Learning about Victoria's past had brought things into perspective for me, how she'd had a privileged life, growing up wealthy and beautiful. She wasn't used to hearing no, or having people argue with her. But raising a baby alone had been a burden for her, and when her daughter had fallen sick she had tried to comfort her with toys and ice cream because she didn't know how to help her. She had pushed her family and friends away, including the mother she had mentioned – she had become estranged from them all. When her daughter died, Victoria had disappeared, winding up in our town and deciding to stay. She wanted a new life, and meeting Mark, she'd decided he would be the one for her, and Poppy had cemented the deal – she could make a new family. Poppy looked just like her daughter, and would make a suitable replacement. Patrick, charmed by her beauty, hadn't bothered to check her references and simply believed her lies. It seemed we could all be blind when we were teased with something we desperately wanted.

Instinctively I'd known there was something wrong with Victoria, but the time for gloating and saying "I told you so" had passed. Now all I felt for her was sadness and pity. She'd died lost and alone, the way she'd probably lived for a long time. I was determined now more than ever to keep my family close, and not pressure myself too much to become a parent. If it didn't happen, I had so many people around me to love. I had a husband who loved me, a husband who was enough for me all on his own.

And that was amazing.

Epilogue

Swallowing the last of my coffee, I stared at the calendar. Test day.

Mark and I had only had sex a couple of times, but the compulsion to check had become ingrained. Because what if I didn't and I finally got that positive result? I knew I wouldn't, I was resigned to the fact, but I couldn't let today pass without knowing for sure.

In the bathroom, I withdrew a pregnancy test from the stash in the bottom drawer. After going to the toilet, I washed my hands and leaned against the sink. I didn't clean, I didn't need to keep my hands busy. The waiting didn't seem so agonising right now, so I stood, held my face up to the sun, and just breathed.

The alarm on my phone finally sounded, and I picked up the plastic stick.

Negative. As I knew it would be.

I stared at myself in the mirror, but I was okay. I felt numb to the trauma; after all that had happened, trying for a baby didn't hold the same weight as it had. It would be a bonus, really, if our dream came true. But how lucky was I to have someone like Mark by my side, when so many women who wanted children were alone. When someone like Victoria went through what she did and was left broken by it?

I flicked the plastic stick into the bin.

Acknowledgements:

Firstly, a huge thanks to my editor, Amanda, for your invaluable advice once again. You made this book so much better.

Thank you to Rebekah at Vivid Covers for the beautiful cover – it's perfect!

I am also indebted to Nick Lefebvre for the firefighting information, Melissa Lefebvre for the medical help, and those special people who read drafts and offered suggestions.

I am so lucky to have a family who loves and supports me. Thank you to Mum and Dad for your unwavering love and support. Thanks to my brothers and their families for always being there when I need you, and thanks to my nieces and nephews for making me smile every time I see you.

Thanks also to the friends and relatives who ask me how the writing is going, for reading my work, giving me feedback, and recommending my books to others. Your support means the world.

And as always, thanks to Ash for your endless encouragement. You are my great love, and all I'll ever need.

About Brooke:

Brooke Linford is an author and editor from Victoria, Australia.

Her first novel, *Broken*, was published in 2017 and *The Empty Room* followed in 2021.

Broken: Sample

1.

I wanted tonight to be a success, but even as I rushed home, a dark cloud of foreboding settled over me. I'd left work early to make sure my apartment was perfect before my parents arrived. I made the bed with fresh sheets for them to sleep in, and my two fluffiest towels hung in the bathroom. I dug through the back of the pantry for the last few items Mum had given me – a rose-patterned vase and scented candles – and placed them strategically around the room. Hopefully all my preparations meant there'd be no fuel for an argument.

They showed up after an hour of me glancing frequently through the window, watching the darkening street for their Jeep. Finally, my mother swept up the stairs and stepped over the threshold.

She gazed around her, her face falling in dismay. 'Oh, Amanda, I thought you were going to upgrade this lounge suite.'

My heart sank. *Jesus, that's the first thing she says?* Ignoring the comment, I kissed her cheek, and helped Dad wheel in their suitcase.

I'd warned Giovanni and Marianne we were coming to Alberto's for dinner, and I was already dressed and ready, tapping my fingers on the bench top as my parents settled into my bedroom.

'I don't even know how you're going to get through the night on that thing,' Mum called through the bedroom curtain I'd strung between the two rooms. I heard the spray of a perfume bottle, and a moment later a heavy floral scent filled the air. 'That couch is so old. You'll wake up crippled in the morning.'

A series of snappy retorts wound through my mind, but I bit them all back. Dad sat beside me on the sagging leather couch and raised his eyebrows at me, adding a calm smile – I couldn't figure out how he managed it.

'Are you really wearing that?' Mum asked, wrinkling her nose.

She looked trim and elegant in a charcoal woollen skirt, her cardigan matching perfectly. She'd reapplied her makeup, and not a strand of her shiny hair was out of place. I surveyed my own outfit; I'd chosen it carefully, I thought. I'd tossed aside everything else, finally settling on this combination.

'What do you mean?' I asked.

'*This.*' She plucked at the sleeve of my red leather jacket with two manicured fingernails. 'Where did you get this?'

'It's Marianne's,' I murmured, feeling the familiar prickle of irritation run across my scalp.

'That girl has always had questionable fashion sense.'

Her face puckered in disgust. It was no secret my mother and my best friend couldn't stand each other. Sighing, I shrugged off the jacket and slid on a plain black cardigan instead. What was the point of arguing?

Dad flicked through a tattered magazine on the coffee table, ignoring the tension in the room.

*

Peak-hour traffic was still heavy by the time we arrived at the restaurant. I jumped off the tram and tried to walk ahead of my parents, but my mother kept me back with a barrage of criticism.

'... I'm just saying that it wouldn't hurt to look at other places to live. You don't even have a security code on the building, and your front door doesn't shut properly. Don't think I didn't notice that.'

The warm light of Alberto's spilled gently through the windows ahead. I focused on it as we neared; the sound of Mum's high heels hammering on the footpath pounded against my skull.

'And with winter coming, I can't believe you haven't spoken to your landlord about the heating. It shouldn't be up to you to buy your own electric heater. They cost a fortune to run, you know. Honestly, you need to get on to that. You're cold, and you're in a building with no security. I mean, what if someone breaks in? A rapist could walk right up to your door–'

'We're here.' I barged through the door into the crowded restaurant. The clatter washed over me – voices, cutlery scraping plates, music – and instantly I felt calmer. I released a long breath.

'You won't have to help out tonight, will you?' Mum

asked as she squeezed past me.

'No, Mum, I don't work here anymore.'

'I just want to have a nice relaxing meal with my birthday girl, that's all,' she said into my ear. I almost smiled. Maybe if she stopped talking about how shit my place was then I could relax for a minute.

I found our reserved table – my regular table – and led my parents towards it. People surrounded the bar and Giovanni greeted them effortlessly as he passed by.

'*Ciao, carina*,' he cooed, scooping me into his arms. I rested my cheek against the cool silk of his shirt. 'And here they are,' he said, reaching out to my parents. 'Welcome, it has been so long since we saw you last here.'

My mother frowned, concentrating on untangling Giovanni's accent. Finally her red-painted lips curled into a hesitant smile.

'Thank you.' Dad nodded as he shook hands with Giovanni.

'Have you met Lucas yet, our new barista?' Giovanni asked me, his eyes shining.

Oh God, here we go. 'Not yet.' I kept my tone light, aware that Mum was listening hard. 'How's Luisa? Is she here tonight?'

He shook his head. '*Stanca.*' He glanced up at my parents and held his hands in front of his belly.

'Oh,' my mother sighed. 'Your wife is pregnant?'

'*Si*, our second baby. Due in four weeks.'

Mum's face lit up, and she looked at me with a smile. *Tick tock,* I could almost hear her say.

'Is Marianne in the kitchen?' I asked.

'*Si*,' Giovanni replied. 'Go, go.' He flicked his hand,

slipping into my chair as I stood.

Marianne ladled sauce over a steaming mound of pasta. Her whites were stained red, her hair pulled back tight, and she wore a mask of determination. 'Helena!' she barked as I leaned against the bench, watching her work.

I missed the hustle of the restaurant, the smell of beer under my fingernails, the music and drinks at the end of the night while we slopped water across the floors. Working as a receptionist just wasn't the same.

I should have left the kitchen and rescued my parents from Giovanni's small talk, but I'd promised Marianne I'd let her know when we arrived. She wanted to be prepared for my mother – who she hated like poison – and she was desperate for me to meet Lucas, the barista. She'd been raving about him for weeks.

She kissed my forehead. 'You're here. How's it going?' She pushed her damp hair behind her ears. I knew what *it* meant.

'She's been her usual self.' I forced a smile. 'You know, my place lacks security, the heating thing ... and apparently I'm under threat of a rapist breaking through my door.'

'Christ,' Marianne moaned. 'You've lived alone for years. You lived alone in Italy, for fuck's sake–'

'Yeah, yeah.' I nodded, interrupting before she got carried away. 'Busy tonight, hey.'

She shrugged, surveying the kitchen. 'That reminds me, can you help me prep tomorrow arvo? We've got the Desio family coming in for dinner.'

'All of them?'

'Yeah, a birthday party.'

'That's fine.'

She slapped the bench top. 'Oh God, wait, have you met him yet?'

'Lucas?' I took a deep breath, pushing away my irritation. 'No, not yet.'

'God, he's so perfect for you.'

I chuckled. 'The poor guy.'

'Where is he? He was just out here on a break.' She went to the kitchen door and peered through. 'Here. Quick!' She beckoned me over. 'You didn't see him at the bar?'

'I didn't, but my mum's here and Giovanni has an accent.'

She rolled her eyes. 'Well, Lucas started three weeks ago, you know. I can't believe you haven't been here for *three weeks.*' She pointed.

'I've been busy ...' I murmured. *And putting off this forced fix-up for as long as possible.*

At the end of the bar, Lucas worked in a cloud of steam behind the coffee machine. He was tall, thin, with long blond hair pulled back into a messy ponytail, his white sleeves rolled up to the elbows. Marianne had already worked her way into his life, and she'd been spoon-feeding me morsels of information ever since.

I knew he'd walked in off the street, desperate for work. I knew he was a trained barista who planned to source and roast his own beans one day; that he couldn't speak a word of Italian but loved Italian food. I knew, even though she hadn't told me, that Marianne had convinced Giovanni to hire him. I knew what her argument would have been – Giovanni's wife Luisa was about to give birth, and they needed someone to replace her, someone who could make coffee as great as Luisa. And I knew, by the sparkle in his eye earlier, that Giovanni was now on board to set the two of us up.

Marianne was convinced we would hit it off and that if I relaxed and went with it then ... what? All my troubles would disappear? She was sketchy on that last part.

I leaned back against the door jamb as Helena the waitress wobbled past with a pile of dirty plates. 'You know, I do have a life outside of this place,' I whispered to Marianne, who studied me carefully. 'So, what have you told him about me?'

Marianne grinned. 'Just do me a favour,' she whispered. 'Order yourself a coffee.'

I nudged her back into the hot kitchen. 'Shit, now you've made me nervous,' I said, louder now my voice had to compete with kitchen noise.

'Isn't he kind of stunning though?' Marianne mused.

'I have to get back out there,' I said, shaking my head. 'And you know you have to come talk to my mother.'

Marianne jabbed a finger at my chest. 'Just don't leave me alone with her.'

*

We ate *baccala*, crab risotto, and drank Prosecco and beer. Dad toasted me for my upcoming birthday and for a brief shining moment I was content in their company. It was a rare occurrence, and I knew that on some level I still wanted their approval; for them to be proud of me, treat me like an adult, and enjoy spending time with me. I would never admit that to Marianne.

Giovanni floated back and forth, joining us for a drink and charming my parents. Once Mum was tipsy enough to practice her basic Italian greetings on him, I took the opportunity to introduce myself to Lucas.

'You're Amanda,' he said, before I'd even opened my mouth. I raised my eyebrows in reply. 'Marianne pointed you out.'

'Yep, she's been wording him up,' Pete the barman called, stacking glasses into a rack beneath the bar.

'It's good to meet you, anyway,' Lucas said. The blue lights behind the bar cast him in an eerie glow that made my breath catch. Glancing towards the kitchen, I was pleased that Marianne wasn't spying at least. She was right about one thing; he was kind of stunning.

'You too.' Taking a breath, I shoved my hands into my jeans pockets. 'Apparently you make great coffee.'

He beamed. 'Well, what can I get for you?'

'A latte would be great.'

'What about your parents?' He lifted his chin in their direction and I looked over my shoulder. Mum threw her head back and cackled at something Giovanni said.

Oh God, she's pissed. 'I think they're fine.'

I made small talk with Pete and tried not to stare at Lucas while he prepared my coffee; hunching over the cup, swirling the milk into a feather pattern. He nudged the cup across the bar and waited, arms crossed, while I took a sip.

'It's very good.'

He grinned. 'You have a great blend here.'

I smiled back. Pete edged closer along the bar to watch our exchange. I cleared my throat, aware that everything I said or did was being scrutinised. It was warm in the restaurant, and I fought the instinct to fan my face. 'You like it here?'

'Yeah, everyone's been great.' He flicked a glance at Pete, who whipped a tea towel out of his belt and started wiping down the bar. 'By the way, Marianne invited me to the barbecue for your birthday ...'

A flutter in my tummy. *Damn you, Marianne.* 'Okay, no worries.'

'Well, she's met my housemate Cam and they've hit it off, so she's asked him too.'

I forced a nonchalant smile. *I suck at this.* 'That's fine.'

An awkward silence fell between us. People waited behind me, but Pete hadn't seemed to notice them. I picked up my cup and saucer and shrugged, relief coursing through me that this first meeting was finally over.

'We'll talk more on Sunday, then,' Lucas said.

I nodded. 'Thanks for the coffee.'

*

Outside, the breeze snapped its teeth against my skin. Mum was still tipsy, and as we stepped onto the street, she collided with a man in a black trench coat. Instead of being embarrassed, she wrapped her painted fingernails around his sleeve, cooing, 'Well, hello there!'

He tore his arm free, disgust stark on his face.

'Sorry,' I murmured, trying to tug Mum away. His eyes slid over to me, and his mouth twisted into a sneer. My stomach clenched and I grabbed Mum again, making her stumble. 'Come on,' I hissed, yanking her behind me.

'That's the type of man you want to find, Amanda,' she said loudly as we turned to follow Dad. He was whistling on ahead, strolling towards the tram stop with his hands in his pockets. 'Not some boy with long hair who makes coffee for a living.'

I increased my pace. Adding alcohol to my mother's already insufferable personality was such a bad idea.

'Now he might be fun, but you need to get yourself a real man.'

'Oh, Jesus, you're drunk, Mum.'

'No really,' she cried, adding a shrill giggle. 'Did you see the suit on that guy? Now, he has money, and that's important. Security is important, you know that.'

Glancing over my shoulder, I saw the man lingering outside the door to Alberto's, watching us walk away. His stare made my stomach turn. *What's his problem?* The man stood eerily still. A muffled ringtone escaped his suit but he ignored it, simply staring after us as I hurried my mother along.

'I'm not really looking for a relationship right now,' I said, fighting a shudder.

'So you keep telling me.' The toe of her shoe scuffed the pavement, tripping her a little. I caught her shoulders, straightening her out.

'Then maybe you should start listening to me.' I nudged her ahead of me. 'Come on, Dad's waiting.'